I0666532

University and King

By Jeffery Ryan Long

Agnes Publishing

Honolulu, Hawaii
2014

Published in the USA by Aignos Publishing, Inc.
1910 Ala Moana Blvd, #20A
Honolulu, HI 96815
www.aignospublishing.com

Printed in the USA

Edited by Zachary M. Oliver
Cover art provided by Bryce Watanabe
Design by Liang-Han "Kevin" Yu

13-digit ISBN: 978-0-9895191-5-1
10-digit ISBN: 0989519155

This book is fictional; no character portrayed in this story is intended to be based on or having originated on any actual living person known by the author or any individual involved in the publishing of this novella.

The author and publisher have neither liability nor responsibility to any person or entity with respect to any loss or damage caused, or alleged to have been caused, directly or indirectly, by the information conveyed in this book.

Aignos Publishing
Honolulu, Hawaii
2014

For my friends

University and King

Table of Contents

"Two Drunks" previously published in *Intellectual Refuge*
"Defender" previously published in *Hawai'i Review*
"Executioner in the Lunchroom" previously published in *Arcadia*
"Honolulu Labyrinth Society" previously published in *Labyrinth Inhabitant*
"Waikiki Wedding" previously published in *Euphemism*
"The Ala Wai at Night" previously published in *SAND*
"R.O.E." previously published in *The Fine Line*

Before the phantom of False morning died,
Methought a Voice within the Tavern Cried

--Edward FitzGerald
The Rubaiyat of Omar Khayyam

Two Drunks

Two drunks were thrown out of a cab on King Street just outside of Star Market, the drunk riding shotgun having painted a red, fan-shaped smear of barf on the outside of the car door, just below the open window. When the taxi stopped and the driver said "get out, get the hell out of my cab" both drunks only understood that "Put a Little Love in Your Heart" had been playing over the radio, and now it wasn't. The drunk in the back pulled himself forward by the headrests of the front two seats, his fingers brushing the back of the driver's neck.

"What happened to the tunes?" he asked the driver.

The drunk in the front coughed outside the window and the sound of a large splatter was audible in the after burn of the Honda Civic gassing past them.

"Your friend is messing up my cab. Get him out of here."

The one in the back blinked for a few moments. Some animal's cunning cut to the top of his foaming, outraged brain with its rat's teeth and said "Do not piss this man off." So instead of what might have been an inconvenient episode of bloody noses and police, the drunk mitigated his spluttering indignity into spluttering remorse. Apology after apology fell out of his mouth so naturally it seemed he'd been saying "I'm sorry" his whole life. Which he had.

The drunk in back paid the fare with a substantial tip that rounded off what remained of his last paycheck to an even twenty dollars. He had a dim awareness he wouldn't see the cab fare again, especially paid in recompense by the nearly unconscious drunk in front. Speaking of whom had just settled into his seat, wiped the back of his hand across his mouth and said softly, "That feels a whole lot better."

And as the eyes of the drunk in front closed, the one in back opened his door and pulled him by his arm to his feet on the street-lit sidewalk.

"What?" the drunk said, and the other drunk said, "Just shut up and close the door." He smiled and waved to the driver, who had already placed his passengers outside his consciousness and stared hard at the windshield until the two drunks were clear. With an inspiring display of dignity the cab driver pulled away slowly, then force-fed them rubber smoke from his squealing rear tires before rocket-launching to the next red light.

It was now only the two drunks with the dead cars in the Star Market parking lot reflecting white street lamps above them. The rest of the surrounding world,the health food store, the Subway sandwich shop across the street, and the park with its towering orange gateway memorial,might just as well have been the blank unreachable universe that had hung over their heads for all of their lives, as much interest or even cognizance had they of it, of anything not liquid and not directly in front of them.

"Looks like we're walking," one drunk said to the other. One cab an evening was expensive enough—two cab rides was a fairytale. Two cab rides in one evening was the same as wearing jeweled crowns and fur. The buses had all stopped running.

"Magoo's is up the road," the other drunk said to the

first. Wobbling in place, he leaned forward as if he could see through the haze the industrial bulbs threw all over the place. As it was, he could see as far as the perimeter of the parking lot. "One beer and we're done."

Each of the two drunks was drunk in his own way, but from one moment to the next each drunk experienced a constant sliding into the other's psychology of drunkenness. It hardly mattered that one was a bit stouter than the other, one had more hair than the other, one wore a t-shirt while the other wore a polo shirt, one wore jeans and rubber slippers and the other wore khaki shorts and tennis shoes. Or that one drank because for the greater part of the day he'd had no opportunity to say what he really thought about anything in general or in particular; all of his feelings except an enthusiasm for industriousness and a bland friendliness to colleagues was promptly censored lest it expose him as a libertine or an insurrectionist, which he was at heart. And it hardly mattered that the other drunk exhausted himself daily in an attempt to make people who had no affection and little respect for him do exactly what they did not want to do — data entry, time sheets, payroll — so that the results he could identify in his labors was a common misery shared by everyone he was doomed to supervise. The characteristics that distinguished one drunk from the other vanished as the evening progressed. Each drunk's drunkenness intensified into a frenzy complementary to the other by beer after beer, whiskey after whiskey. And the bars were all the same — the Varsity, which the drunks still referred to as Magoo's, was the same as Anna Bananna's, was the same as On Stage, was the same as Champions and 8 Fat Fat 8.

At the beer garden they called Magoo's the two drunks repeated the cycle that had occurred at the other places, that had occurred between all drunks since the first Egyptian drank fermented honey from an owl's skull and got his bosom friend involved in the discovery. The cycle that would continue until the world was only a forest of mushroom clouds.

There was a false demureness, coupled with a barely concealed hostility, shown to the bald and bearded bouncer slouching over his podium at the front, which was plastered with posters of sweaty beer bottles. It was the same attitude they'd shown and would show to all bouncers and bartenders who checked ID's either on general principles or because they were dickheaded enough to think that the drunks weren't over twenty-one (which both were by about ten years).

After the entrance was the survey of the room for attractive girls, the buying of drinks, the taking of seats at a vantage point suitable for blatant eye-balling. And so the cycle continued, with the language growing coarser and louder, with the f-word and "douchebag" falling in front of every third declaration. At one point, the sound system would play a song that would make both drunks shut up for a moment, each awash in a maudlin and completely fabricated sentiment provoked by the all-too-clear image of a love who had left him precisely because he was who he was and could not, in all probability, be anyone else. At these moments, the drunks' clarity of vision would shine a light inward to the shapes in their hearts, mostly populated by all they ever wanted and did not get or everything they'd thrown away. Perhaps it was Marvin Gaye that night, or Sam Cooke or Mariah Carey or the Spin Doctors. One of the drunks felt stabbed in the chest by his finer feelings—feelings that, when even only lightly applied, go all the way in and through the other side— feelings only a poet has the suicidal nature to express. But this drunk had only the limited ability to express his sweet pain with the tonality and articulation of a simpering baby.

"That's the way it goes, I guess," one drunk said.

"It doesn't matter," the other drunk said, really believing that it mattered a damn bunch.

After the gauche and (to risk redundancy for emphasis) maudlin sentiments had been exchanged, the inappropriate comments about people they didn't know bubbled out of their mouths, the singling out of an individual made oblivious recipient to their mounting rage — "that goddamn douchebag, who the hell does he think he is? Look at that stupid asshole, just sit down already and get out of my line of sight" — their anger buffered and given nuance by the small indignities at work and at the hands of friends and family. On this night a tall, dark-haired girl entered after they'd sat down and took a table with a male friend not far from theirs. One of the drunks closed his mouth and simmered — at some time, at some bar, the other drunk had convinced him to ask for the girl's number and he'd done it. She'd given it to him, and he'd left ridiculous text messages on her phone asking her to the movies, to which she'd never responded. Now he stared at her thinking she ought to come up and talk to him in person. The other drunk alternated between telling the first drunk to forget about her and inciting him to go talk to her again. This went on until someone yelled last call, and the lights blinked off and on.

As it always was, the two drunks did not recall buying chili nachos or hot dogs at 7-11, but the nachos and hot dogs were in their right hands with Gatorades in their left hands, and it didn't matter who ate what because one of them had eaten nachos and the other had eaten hot dogs and vice versa, hundreds of times before, and would continue to do so until hot dogs and chili nachos ceased to exist. When, in the grainy dimness of the freeway underpass towards Kapahulu and Kaimuki, one of the drunks realized that nachos and Gatorade were in his hands a couple of blocks away from 7-11, he pulled back like a pitcher and flung the nachos into the street and, after it, the capped drink that was unbearably moist and slick in his palm. A burst followed the touchdown, the giving way of liquid encased in plastic to asphalt and grit.

"What are you doing?" the other drunk said.

But by this time the first drunk, with exhaustion sweeping aside intoxication and a manic sobriety pulling at his conscience as if trying to open a locked door, could only muster up mumbled curses to his enemies in response. He stepped forward uncertainly, but stepped forward nonetheless along the running stream that he crossed and disregarded. Now he was too tired to invent something to drop into the black water undulating with milky white spots, reflections of the world above him.

The other drunk shrugged, followed, and ate.

They had a long walk to the end of Kaimuki, most of it uphill. Though they'd made this drunken stroll over and over again they did not consider the most expedient route—all that existed was the way forward, no matter how strenuous or slow.

On Lincoln Avenue, just outside the bottom level of Market City Mall, one drunk recalled, for reasons unbeknownst to rational minds, that the other had been stonewalled by the girl he pretended to be in love with. And he really was, no matter how tawdry and tarnished and desperate the sum of his love now was. During empty moments at work, the other drunk had imagined walks on desolate beach walls, along strange coasts, illuminated by the constant richness of a late afternoon sun. He envisioned a proposal, an acceptance, a shared household, a child, a long uninteresting existence shared with this woman. It was the same fantasy he had managed since he first loved a woman, except the faces had changed and the details had become so exacting as to be perverse. This other drunk would have to wait for another face, another transparent vessel into which to dump his unattainable dream life.

"Too bad about whatzername," one drunk said to the other from behind. "Well, forget her anyways."

The other drunk had reached the dead ends of every feeling he held in his heart. His nervous system had been broken down into its basic components, and now he was simply acting upon vague memories of thoughts or feelings — hardly the thoughts or feelings themselves.

"I'm not mad at her," he replied, not knowing what

would happen as he approached the *Honolulu Star-Advertiser* dispenser that stood outside the front door of Sekiya's Japanese restaurant. "I'm pissed off at the guy who told me to ask for her number in the first place." With that, he grasped the locked head of the newspaper machine and pulled it face down to the sidewalk, and scraping, slamming metal reverberated through the park behind them. He then continued the walk up Lincoln.

"Pick that up," one drunk said.

"Fuck that," the other drunk said.

"Pick that shit up," one drunk said.

The other drunk, with neither chagrin, nor remorse, nor resentment, lifted the newspaper machine from where it lay and set it back in its place next to the *Honolulu Star-Bulletin*. He continued the walk up Lincoln.

Later, they somehow moved off Lincoln Avenue, via a walking bridge over the freeway. They discovered themselves on Pahoa Street, the night world powered by the street lights' garish imitation of day, the hills painted in suburban orange and green and brown and dirt red. What had been a steady incline to Kokohead Avenue — their destination was a block past the fire station — was now an excruciating slope of Alpine proportions. One drunk suddenly had enough, and just before he went down to one knee and then fell on his back on the soft, clipped lawn of a stranger's house, he tore off the shirt he'd tied to his head and flung it toward the street.

The other drunk collected the shirt and dropped it next to the collapsed drunk's body. "We're almost there."

"We're *not* almost there," the drunk said. "I'm just gonna sleep for a second."

"You're not sleeping for a second," the other drunk said.

The drunk on the ground saw only an enveloping blackness as soft as the ground beneath his back and wanted nothing but to surrender, to let go of all the shit he'd been through this night, all the shit of his entire life. He had at last made it beyond the point of love and rage and if only this could be what life felt like from now on, he could bear it. He could even excel. As it was, it was too hard feeling so many things all the time. It was too hard not having the people around who might have listened to what he had to say. Sleep now and he could forget, and start completely over in the morning.

"You're gonna regret it if you pass out here."

The drunk opened his eyes and looked up at the other drunk, whose face in shadow had lost its tightness and now looked like loose, dark cloth hanging from the front of his skull. The other drunk swayed slightly above the drunk on the ground and held out a swaying hand. The drunk took it, pulled himself to his knees, then his feet, and the two drunks took the hill up into Kaimuki with the faltering steps of an elderly couple. Self-abnegation, in its most sublime sense, had reduced their collected psychologies to a temporary zero, and they found their way home like dogs at the end of an incredible journey.

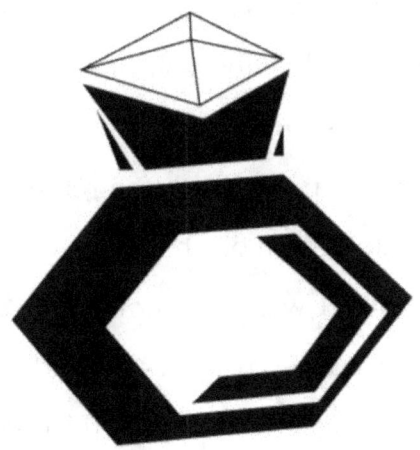

Defender

Every day I think about Shaun Francisco and what I'm doing with his wife.

My roommates don't know, would probably care less if they did. That's the best thing about these people.

When we're all around the television set—Dave on his fold-out mattress, Aaron in the wicker seat, Cindy next to me on the sofa—it's startling how close they are, with no awareness of who I am or what I've done. When I'm standing in the kitchen eating a bowl of cereal over the counter, and Aaron walks in for his Triscuits—or when I pass Cindy on her way to the bathroom and say good morning, or when Dave places a Dos Equis on the table as I'm reading *The New Yorker* under the good light—I'm amazed at how we've all learned to live together with our pasts blank, no reference point beyond the shapes of our clothes on our bodies.

No one knows I was complimented for my thick head of hair, that I drove a foreign sports car and went to work in a pressed suit, that my wife was dead at thirty-three. They don't even know I had a wife. What I appear to them now—a former alcoholic, maybe, a washout, barely scraping by— makes far more sense than who I was before. They might assume that I had, at one point in my life, a nervous breakdown. I was Public Defender for the State. I spent years failing to protect the ruined lives of men guilty beyond a doubt.

Every day I think about Shaun Francisco and what I'm doing with his wife.

But I saw his wife take off her ring and give it to the prison guard while Shaun cried on the other side of the glass.

On the television, a dad calls his son a dumbass and my roommates laugh. I pretend to laugh in the same way. I don't follow jokes all that well anymore. I have a hard time answering questions, too. I can talk well enough, but as soon as someone asks me something—I don't know—I can't say anything. I'm wondering what they want to hear.

My roommates laugh again, but now I'm too uptight. Side effects. Living in this kind of environment, this anonymous good will, is comforting sometimes. But sometimes it makes you feel like you don't exist and never did.

Lehua calls, says she'll get me in twenty minutes. When I hear her voice disembodied over the tiny phone speaker I'm here again, I'm real again, and all of a sudden I feel like the sum of something more than just the bland and easygoing fellow I play in this house. All of a sudden I've got a dick and prejudices and a sense of righteous wrath. I slide past the backs of my roommates' heads with my plastic Safeway bag of things and close the door softly when I leave. Here, I'm all about not disturbing anything.

Lehua's coming from work—day shift at Big City Diner in Kaimuki. Usually she works Sunday, the breakfast and lunch crowd, but today she switched with someone. I don't know their names. I only know that every one of them, according to Lehua, has a strong and peculiar way of interpreting events in the dining room, constructing a version of reality unto themselves in which they are never wrong but eternally suffering for the iniquities of others. Since she traded shifts we'll have Sunday to spend at the beach with Analyn and Tracey.

And Shaun Francisco's probably rereading Borges on his prison bunk, or bench pressing at the rusty weight set, breathing the sour smell of men always crowding him, taking his fresh air, using his things. While I fuck his wife and play with his kids.

First there will be a ride in the '99 Camry from Manoa to Kalihi, where Lehua will pick up the kids from her mother's house, then to her apartment in Kaneohe—*their* apartment—where I'll lean on what used to be his counter, open his refrigerator, and lie in his bed.

After I get in the car I put the plastic bag between my legs on the floorboard. She's smiling with her sunglasses on, and it takes me a few seconds to understand I should kiss her. I can taste her whole rotten day over her lips.

"That plastic bag again," she says, pulling onto Oahu Road. "Why don't you let me buy you a backpack or something?"

"Well," I say. There are actually several reasons why I don't buy a backpack, good reasons, but faced with her stark question each careful explanation buries itself under dirt, under lead, under a substance it would take impossible amounts of time and effort to displace.

"Never mind," she says, freeing one hand from the

wheel to stroke my cheek.

"Dave was really on a roll today," I say, pulling the windshield shade down over the descending sun.

"Oh," she says noncommittally. She knows how to communicate with me. I lose my voice when the stakes are high.

"This time it was about *Eyes Wide Shut*. Stanley Kubrick dead before the film was released. Apparently, he got too close to how rich people really spend their money — prostitutes at ritual mask parties, stuff like that. It turns out they assassinated him. Those kinds of parties happen all the time at this place on the Russian River, those mask parties — and it all goes back to the Skull and Bones Club, where the initiation for new members is to have sex in a coffin with the disinterred bones of Geronimo."

"Wow," Lehua says.

"I guess there's documents from a certain Indian nation demanding the return of the bones from the head of that fraternity, or whatever it is." Dave's catch phrase — *it's all documented*. Mostly on obscure court transcripts, decades old, reproduced on internet sites.

Lehua's day, she tells me, is populated by the kinds of ingrates I've found reappear in all of her tales of the restaurant. Ghost stories, mostly — old men and women doomed to return to the same local diner weekly, despite never being satisfied with the food and their hatred and hostility towards the wait staff. In different tellings these restaurant daemons change shape, inhabit new bodies, wear new faces, each model invariably older and grumpier.

"Three orders of eggs before the flabby windbag finally thought they were runny enough, but not too runny. All this back and forth from the kitchen in a room full of customers. I wanted to punch her head."

"Eggs—they're a tricky business."

"They're not a tricky business. She made them a tricky business. 'Eh, you know what over-medium means, or what?' What the fuck? Of course I don't know what over-medium means because it doesn't mean shit. There are two types of eggs—hard and easy. All that ambivalent shit doesn't exist to me."

"It's the system that's flawed," I say.

The other characters in her ongoing tragedy are the fat teenagers ordering sundaes for dessert after a breakfast of French toast, the babies flinging mushed-up pancakes into her hair from the high chair, the low-carb dieters, the carnivores, the vegetarians who refuse to eat around the meat, the ones who don't want beans in the chili, the loners with their open papers, the Bloody Mary crowd. They are all vessels for her contempt. Their roles are interchangeable.

I wait in the car while Lehua talks to her mother. Analyn and Tracey race out of the front door as if they've just eaten a whole birthday cake, their sugar-filled mania bordering on bloodlust. As soon as I spot them near the car I roll up the windows and lock the doors.

Analyn, at six, a year older than her sister, tries the handle. "Open, Uncle, open up, open up!" She moves to the back door and I point to my ears, pretending not to hear.

Tracey mimics her sister's every move and when they've tried all the doors they stand level with my head and pound their open palms on the glass. "Open up! Open up!" they scream, while on the other side of the window I put my hands together under my cheek, pretending to sleep.

When Lehua opens the door Tracey nearly tackles Analyn into the wide back seat. "Hey, you guys," I say. "I didn't notice you out there."

"We're girls, not guys," Analyn shouts, still not in full control of her voice. Then a hand comes from behind the headrest and cups my throat, and another on my cheek near my nose, another on my ear, another at my forehead.

"Uncle, Uncle," they cry, pulling the skin on my face back.

"Hey—hey! Cut that out. You folks sit back and buckle

those seat belts." Lehua looks over the rim of her sunglasses at them, her body twisted around in the driver's seat. "You want Uncle to play *Rainbow Magic* with you? Huh?"

Rainbow Magic. A game board in pink, built-in failsafe so there are no losers. The printed words along the checkered track are big enough for me to see without my glasses.

After a dinner of boneless chicken breasts and macaroni and cheese we play the game. My wishes come true, just as everyone else's do, when I make it to the end. Then Lehua and I put on Winnie the Pooh for them in bed—I play Eeyore and Piglet. The two of us shower together, and she kisses me while I lather her breasts and nipples and her Caesarean scar. Warm water falls hard over our bodies and we embrace.

I turn from my side to my back on the damp sheets, breathing hard, laughing. "Oh my god," I say, throwing my arm over my head.

"Why are you laughing," Lehua says, poking me. "Don't try to answer that." Nuzzling at my neck, the motion of her chin and lips and nose vibrating upwards—she breathes lightly in my ear, and through the whoosh of wind I hear a soft "I love you."

I turn towards her face and close my eyes. Every declaration of love is followed by an unspoken question, an implied request for a response. "I love you—*do you love me?*"

The question now lies dormant between silent ellipses, but I can see it through my closed eyes hanging above the bed as if illuminated in neon.

I know she's looking at me, waiting. Instead of acknowledging the bright quiet question, I open my eyes and it disappears.

The next morning I wake up while Lehua sleeps. Before I get into my boxers, I go through my bag, carefully, but the plastic still crackles and hisses. Under my surf shorts and my second-hand Kinko's shirt are my keys, my wallet, some pennies and dimes — but the pills aren't there. I lay out every item on the floor, open, unfolded, flattened out, every card removed from the slots in my wallet. Standing above the assembled pieces of evidence I conclude my medication is certainly not there, that it remains on the top of the dresser in my closet next to a pile of folded jeans. Maybe it's no big deal. I've gone a day or two without pills before. But I can't, not this time, not with Lehua — we'll just have to drive back to Manoa when she wakes up.

Or is this a test? To see if I can maintain without the drugs?

If I can hold it all together?

After I dress, I sneak into the kitchen as I did on the weekends when Rebecca was alive. She was the kind of person that could enjoy sleep, while I needed facts to flow through my head continuously, terrified I'd forget them. Rebecca also enjoyed a long, drawn out Sunday breakfast, on the one day she didn't care what she put in her mouth. The whole week she'd punish herself with bran twigs and soy milk and grapefruit, just so on Sunday she could relish waffles, pancakes, spam and eggs, loco mocos, fried rice, whatever I'd bought the day before. I'd watch her face over the *Advertiser* as she languorously slid each greasy, sticky bite from the tines of her fork with her teeth. When the dishes were done we'd wreck our stomachs with a whole pot of French Roast between the two of us and talk for an hour about whether to go to the beach, the movies, or the mall.

I pull Lehua's big pan from the dish drainer and set it on the stove. There's maple syrup in the refrigerator, which leads to the thought of pancakes — but inside the flour jar are the brown corpses of suffocated insects.

Having scrounged a half-loaf of Love's King White, four eggs, cinnamon and sugar, I heat the pan and slide a square of Blue Bonnet over the Teflon surface. Tracey and Analyn, in large t-shirts (their father's shirts?) come into the kitchen as I drop the second piece of dripping bread into the pan.

"Are you making breakfast?" Analyn says.

"Uncle is making breakfast!" Tracey shouts. There's one of them at each of my legs. "It smells good!"

"This isn't for you. It's for me and your mommy." I flip a brown, butter-soggy slice onto a plate. "You kids are getting gruel and Brussels sprouts for breakfast."

"What's gruel?" Tracey says, jumping to get a better view of the plate on the counter.

"Uh," I say.

"Oh, Eddie, you're making French toast!" Lehua says, coming up from behind to kiss me on the cheek. "You didn't have to—"

"A good, solid breakfast equips us to deal with the excruciating pain of a new day," I recite, a line from my long-gone marriage. As an addendum, I turn down to look at the children. "When you get older, you'll learn that life is, essentially, a misery." But now Analyn and Tracey are pulling on the sleeves on each other's shirts, each one trying to drag down the other.

"Oh stop it," Lehua says. "Analyn. Tracey. Go get into your swimsuits while Uncle finishes your breakfast. After we eat we'll go."

"The beach, the beach!" they cry, in unison but not in harmony, and they hop out of the kitchen to their rooms.

I decide it's unnecessary after all to take a trip to Manoa

for pills.

#

Lehua rubs sunscreen on the girls' shoulders and backs while I cover our store-bought lunch with my shirt and lay out my towel. "Come with us," she says, as Tracey and Analyn break from our place and run full speed into the gentle shore break.

"No—I'm going to lie in the sun a while. I want to be nice and tan for my interview tomorrow."

"That's right, your interview," she says. "I still don't know why you need to get a job right now."

"It'll be good for me," I say. "It's something to do. And it will bring in some extra money."

"Just keep talking and don't let them ask you any questions," Lehua says. She kisses me and I watch her adjust the seat of her bikini from behind as she steps from the wet sand into the foam. The way each cheek of her ass wobbles with each footfall—immediately I feel the welling of an old guilt, guilt in eternal rising and recession. I squint against the flat, scarred ocean. For a moment, every black dot against the blue glare is Shaun Francisco.

When I saw her take off her ring in front of her husband I had come to O triple C to visit him, as a friend, since I was all used up as his lawyer. I tried to visit all the convicts who'd been clients — all the ones who hadn't been shipped to the mainland, who didn't want to kill me for not getting them off. Shaun wanted to see his babies, but Lehua wasn't about to bring them to the prison. He wasn't going to see them for eight to ten years.

After she left the room I took a seat in front of the glass, looking at Shaun with his hands over his face, his fingertips pressed tight at the edges of his newly-shaved hairline.

"I'm sorry," I said into the intercom. He stood up and, wiping his nose, requested the guard to lead him back to his cell.

"Fuck," I said, resenting that Lehua had to pull this stunt now. I was being selfish, but — I needed someone to talk to, and at that point Shaun Francisco was the best friend I had. A month earlier, my wife Rebecca had been thrown fifteen feet from her bicycle while riding home from work — a Forerunner taking a right turn at a red light. When I rushed to the hospital, I couldn't help but think how embarrassed she must have been to put that big knot into traffic. Not until she was buried did I understand she was dead.

After that, despite the influx of important cases that would decide men's futures for five years, ten years, life, I focused on wide blank spaces in the courtroom as judges and lawyers and witnesses spoke. I wasn't eating, sleeping only when I couldn't help it, smoking cigarettes in a lawn chair in front of the house instead of reading up, planning, doing my homework. I thought Shaun Francisco, a man whose life for the past two years had been a tragedy in which, Oedipus-like, he had had full, yet ignorant, control, would be the one person who could understand me.

If he hadn't gone to prison for selling ice while under the influence of his own product, and committing manslaughter of an elderly couple practicing ballroom dancing as he crashed his rust-spotted Cutlass Supreme into their living room, we might have been friends on the outside. Instead, he'd made a decision to provide for his growing family by procuring, packaging, and distributing crystal meth.

He was articulate, well-read, and had an encyclopedic knowledge of jazz music. His father had been a professional musician who played electric guitar with a hapa-haole outfit in the hotels. During his trial, after all that preliminary talk about defenses and statements, we'd talk records and who played on what. It was Shaun who finally articulated the defense for *Bitches' Brew* for me. A guy like that in prison — well, at least now he can play chess and read every book he ever thought about.

The day Lehua gave back her ring, I saw her crying in the corridor as I walked from the visiting area, her back against the white wall, her hand over her eyes. I pulled some napkins I'd kept from my uneaten doughnut and held them out to her.

"Lehua," I said. "I'm sorry —" Out of all the millions of words I'd spoken as Public Defender, those were most frequent.

"I just don't know why he's acting so surprised," she said. "He knew it was coming. He knew it. I told him before, before he — you know — before then I told him 'you cut that shit out or I'm walking, and the girls are coming with me.' But it was always one more time. Just a little more. We didn't even need a little more fucking money."

"I know," I said — I'd heard Shaun's version of events, which was remarkably similar. Unlike her husband, Lehua did exactly what she said she'd do.

"It's not like I don't love him anymore. It's just that — this situation, it's just not *feasible* anymore. His own children are gonna forget what he looks like —"

"Shaun's...a good guy," I said weakly, knowing that this sort of appellation probably would never apply to him again.

"Fuck," Lehua breathed, struggling to suck something stuck up one of her nostrils.

"Look, I don't have to be downtown for a couple of

hours," I said. "You want a cup of coffee or something?"

She blew her nose and looked at me, her eyes clearing, finally noticing my physical—no longer abstract—appearance. "Okay," she said. "Eddie, what happened to you? Your clothes don't fit anymore."

"My wife's dead," I said, finally giving verbal confirmation to what, until then, I had only silently grasped. I took her by the arm and led her to the parking lot.

"Weird how we both—lost someone, like that," she said, looking out the window of the coffee shop. She turned back to me. "Thank you for what you did for Shaun."

"It's my job," I said, sipping the cold remnants at the bottom of my cup.

"No, it wasn't just your job. You treated him like a human being. That was hard for even me."

"Yeah." I looked to the window now, at the reflections of two wrung-out people that had been twisted until there was nothing left in them.

"It must be hard, having a job like yours. Defending guilty people, trying to keep them out of jail."

"They're not all guilty—I mean at least technically. I mean, isn't everyone guilty? But these guys don't get busted for nothing. The cops, the feds, watching them for months. Undercover, setting them up for the sting. This case—I mean from nowhere, they pulled seven guys who testified to buying ice from him. Can you—I'm sorry."

"No. There's nothing we can do about it."

"I wish I could have done more," I said. "I liked the guy."

"I married him."

Two weeks later I lost every case to which I'd been assigned. Defendants had a way of making me personally accountable for their jail time and I began to see my work through their eyes—I'd failed my clients in every possible way. At home there was no one. Soon I had acquired 360-degree vision, seeing my surroundings all at once—the layers of prisons in which I'd placed myself—my clothes, my car, my house, my job. I sold them all, the Lexus, the suits, the home, now barren, and when Rebecca's sister pulled into the driveway, her headlights stripped the darkness from around my sleeping bag on the lawn. She explained, quite calmly, that I'd lost my mind, which seemed perfectly reasonable.

After the hospital and the sessions and the drugs, I had only a surplus of money and my freedom. Everyone thought I'd buy everything back—instead I got a new wardrobe from Goodwill and placed a three hundred dollar deposit, plus first month's rent of six hundred dollars on a room in Manoa, where I wouldn't be alone but could leave when I wanted.

Lehua was the first person I called. In that time, in Shaun Francisco's absence, I'd taken it upon myself to be her protector, her defender from all the shit in the world.

And now I was acting the lover to my friend's wife, the father to his children, despite that they called me "Uncle." Weren't these, of all crimes, capital offenses, worthy of imprisonment?

At lunch time the girls air-dry across the street from the beach on a stained bed sheet laid over the grass, eating sandwiches and chips. Lehua doesn't want them to get sand in their food. I sip at a can of warm iced-tea and watch them—if I mentioned their father, would they know who I was talking about?

Lehua strokes my hair but pulls her hand away quickly. I know she's been watching me, wondering why I'm so quiet, why I stare down every person passing across the field or along the sidewalks, seeing someone who's not there. But she knows better than to ask me any questions. And I know better than to open my mouth because the first words out will be Shaun Francisco. Forgotten in prison. I haven't seen him since—since Lehua gave back her ring. I wouldn't blame him if he killed me when he got out.

At Lehua's that evening I remain planted on the couch while she puts the girls to bed. The television helps, though between the commercials Shaun Francisco walks through the door. He doesn't aim a gun at me, doesn't draw a sword — he looks at me, and in that look I read "TRAITOR" in capital letters, in bold.

"I'm sorry," I say, as usual. "I was just trying to help."

"Fuck you," he says. "You knew exactly what you were doing."

Lehua comes back into the living room in her sleeping tank top and her panties, pulls the remote from my limp grip, and turns off the television.

"You weren't watching that," she says, pulling her legs up under her as she nestles into the couch, resting her head between my neck and shoulder.

"No," I say softly, terrified of the black television screen.

"You must really be nervous about that interview tomorrow," she says.

I haven't thought about it the whole day.

"You'll do fine, Sweetie. Besides, it's no big deal. We don't really need the money."

I don't. But you do. I'll buy the school supplies, the new clothes, the dental insurance. I am the usurper.

"I wish you'd just move out of that house and stay here," she says, her mouth away from her face, her words squirming away eel-like. "I mean, you're already paying rent for this place."

"Jesus Christ!" I shout, springing off the couch. She catches herself from falling over with an arm. "What have you got me into?"

"Eddie—what—"

"What the fuck do you want? Huh? Your husband's in jail for Christ's sake. And here I am, all tangled up in his shit—"

"His shit?"

"I can't—I can't be this. The guy's in prison, and here I am feeding off his life like a goddamn leech. Why don't I just write you a check every month? You can buy whatever you want."

"You think—you think this is all about money?"

I wipe my hand across my face and look around the room at nothing. I've lost the gift of 360-degree vision—all I see is a dark shadow in a cage deep inside me, a ranting, foaming soul no one would hear if I didn't lend him my voice. "I'll do that, I'll write a check. What else am I good for, right? Here I am, stealing someone else's life—"

"You—ass," she hisses, pushing herself off the couch and glaring at me eye to eye. Her mouth opens. No words form. She swivels toward the door, but before she's out of the room she turns back to me.

"Shaun gave up his place in this family when he did what he did." She looks down and a drop of water splatters on the floor. "I didn't want your fucking *help*, Eddie, I wanted you to—" When she goes into her room I barely hear the door close behind her.

The little ape inside me has retired to his pallet on the floor of his cell, leaving me to deal with the consequences of his raving. It seemed so rational saying it. Why would it hurt her so?

I fall into the couch and close my eyes. I should go to her room to apologize. But I'm tired of saying I'm sorry, I'm tired of everything, and in the blissful few seconds before I fall asleep none of it matters to me—not Shaun Francisco, not Rebecca Ramos, not Lehua and the girls. Nothing matters, and finally I can be without thinking about it.

The ride back to Manoa the next morning is silent. I think I'm being wise not to force the situation into a crisis by being bewildered about what I've said. I know what I've done, and to say that person who said those things wasn't me would be the same as saying the night didn't exist, which we both know is false. Every day I think about Shaun Francisco and what I'm doing with his wife. In the end, though, I pray there will be mitigating circumstances.

When she pulls up to the curb outside my house Lehua keeps her foot on the brake, instead of shifting the car into park as she usually does. Usually we spend 15-20 minutes making googly eyes at each other before we part. She's caught by surprise when I don't go for the door handle but suddenly, rather forcefully, twist my body over the upper gear shift and fall into her unprepared arms, my face sinking into her hair scattered over the headrest. The car jerks forward a few inches until her foot finds the brake again.

"I don't want to lose you," I say, burying most of my voice in the upholstery. "I love you."

The weight of the inevitable question falls upon both of us, and I shift, a cramp tightening in my side. Lehua wriggles in discomfort—and I feel the soft pat of her hand at my back. My words, though unanswered, have been accepted.

"Don't let them ask you any questions, Eddie," she says.

When I walk in the door Dave is in the living room, working on his Tesla coil. A wooden box, with a grill built into one of the sides, is the foundation for a glass tower capped with a circular platform ringed with tubes and threaded with wires, standing about chest high. Each of the tubes contains a thin plate of metal and a particular gas— hydrogen, krypton, argon, helium, neon and so on—and when plugged into an electric socket, the machine sends out waves of bio-electric energy to and through the body, supposedly energizing the cells. I told him it sent out good vibes but he got upset.

"Think about all the structures we inhabit through the day, every day," he told me. "Cars, buildings, elevators — and these are all made out of what? Steel and concrete. In the old days, people spent all their time outside. Now we just sit in the air conditioning, jacking off or whatever. By being inside all the time, we can't get the universal energy that's a by-product of the sun's heat, the revolutions of the earth, the rotations of the planets. That's where this machine comes in. Spend three or four minutes in front of it and you'll feel good as new." He wants to market it as a new age health treatment.

But for three months Dave's machine hasn't worked. When I first moved in he switched the thing on after his sales pitch — then a crackle, a loud snap, and nothing.

After I've taken my pills and showered and changed into clothes for the interview (slacks, white shirt), I sit watching him screw a base panel back into place. Several thin bulbs around the circular surface at the top are black inside, burned out.

Dave sets the screwdriver on the coffee table, dusts his hands, and reaches behind the television set for the power bar, which has been plugged to near capacity—the TV, DVD player, VCR, fan, leg massage—and in the last empty outlet he inserts the rubber coated, three-prong plug.

"It won't blow up," I say, but with little confidence. I actually see the glass tower explode into thousands of scattered shards, cutting us both into shreds of skin, stabbing out our eyes. Dave, skeptical of the government to the point of obsessive paranoia, is only a little troubled by the possibility that a large vessel of gas conducting electricity might detonate in our house, disfiguring or killing us. He flips on the switch and, instead of clear sharp darts piercing my chest and face I feel a current move through me, vibrating each bone and blood vessel as it reaches past my body into the space beyond me. There is a shocking sense of displacement, as if the energy moving in has pushed something out of me.

The sound of channeled electricity barely held in check spits and crackles inside the wooden box base—through the grill I see flashes of purple fire. Dave takes up a gas filled rod from the floor and holds it to the tower. A bridge of lightning forms between the rod and the circular platform. His closed fist around the end of the rod pushes it closer, compressing the lightning, and when he pulls back it stretches into thin, fine, spider web lines. The wooden base coughs and the lightning dies—before Dave has the chance to kick it, the machine hiccups twice and the scattered bolts of electricity awaken inside the box once more.

"It doesn't work perfect, but it works," he shouts over the noise.

I've rolled up the legs of my slacks mid-calf in order not to attract cut grass and other species of damp, loose vegetation to the cuffs of my pants as I walk out of Manoa up towards Punahou. It's rained this morning, as it always does, giving the dead refuse of lawnmowers enhanced clinging properties. That there are no sidewalks in this part of Manoa, I think, has partly sabotaged my previous efforts to secure a job—it wasn't until the third interview I realized the cuffs of my pants, as well as my shoes, had been dusted with grass and other lawn detritus, giving the appearance that I've traveled through a swamp from the depths of a forest. With my trusty plastic bag swinging near my knees, I'm soon past the high school and down on the level streets with the buses and traffic.

I cool off on a bench outside the Capitol building, going through my interview monologue once more:

Yes, I'm aware that the duties of an administrative assistant are not comparable to the responsibilities of a Public Defender, but that is exactly what interested me in this position. Not that I'm looking for some easy job, but if you want someone who can do the work, that's me, just look at my education and professional experience. It's right there. Over-qualified? There's really no such thing as over-qualified, I think, because although I do have the qualifications to be a lawyer, I have little, well, maybe some, of the qualifications to be a secretary. I mean administrative assistant. The point is, I'm willing to learn, and it is the opportunity to learn that makes this position so attractive.

In the office I say hello to the receptionist, decline a cup of coffee, and stand stupidly smiling down at her as she phones the person in charge. Shouldn't have eaten two pills this morning—I thought the extra one might make up for the one I didn't take. But of course it never works out that way. My surroundings—all that exists in the world, really, are comfortably distant, as if I'm viewing everything from the other side of a soundproof window. I could shout, flail my arms about, or hold a smile for a full minute and no one would notice.

Two women approach me together. Without looking too hard I know they've been talking out of the sides of their mouths as they come up the corridor to the offices. One's shorter than the other, the taller one younger, and before we enter the conference room to the rear of the cubicles—I hear the swivel of office chair wheels as the secretaries turn from their computer screens to size me up—the tall woman, Shari, suggests I leave my plastic bag at the receptionist's desk.

Automatically I say "No, I'd rather keep it with me," and lead the way to the conference room. But then I lift it up, staring through the milky plastic at my cell phone, keys, pens, address book, and a condensed history I just bought at Rainbows called *The Guns of August*. World War I. I should have given it to the receptionist.

We all sit down facing one another at the ends of a long, wooden meeting table, the projection screen on the opposite wall half-rolled up. I might have liked a cup of coffee. The framed Successories poster depicts Jordan, body splayed in mid-air, rolling the ball off his fingertips over the rim of the basket. "Rise to the occasion."

"As you can see," I begin, "I came in a few minutes early—punctuality is, professionally speaking, one of my most esteemed virtues. And I don't mean just coming to work on time, I mean starting work on time. There's a big difference. Not lallygagging about at the coffeemaker, not checking email or fantasy football scores. In addition, keeping to the subject of time, I make it my mission to honor all deadlines. My productivity, as you may notice when we begin to work together, is not measured according to high and low points plotted in relation to output—rather, it is a high plateau, a series of plateaus increasing in size in relation to evenly administered applications, all of them mastered in a very short while. The spikes in these plateaus would reflect the personal innovations I've made. Performance of tasks would always remain at peak efficiency. If you take a look at my resume, which you have right in front of you —"

"Excuse me for a moment," the younger woman says. The older one nods, and it is suddenly clear that the younger woman is being evaluated on how she will evaluate me. I look to both of them, wanting to help as best I can.

"Yes, of course," I say. My smile drops when I sense that the smile makes them uneasy. "Let me clarify the statement 'peak efficiency —'"

The younger woman flips through my resume, a three-pager, pretending to read it right in front of me. "I look at your resume, and you've got all this experience — you were a lawyer, yes? — and I just have to wonder. Why would you want to work here?"

"Well —" I say, sighing, looking down.

In the past, answers — to any question, rhetorical or empirical — would be delivered into my brain with the speed of light, words exploding out of my mouth brilliantly before I had the chance to even process them. This made me a lawyer. Now, when faced with a question, I find myself doggy paddling in deep space, an impossible distance separating me from those bright answers.

My answer? *I need something with which to justify my existence. I'm still trapped in the Puritan, pre-American ideal of work ethic as a means to emulate God, who made the world in six days. I am lonely a great deal of the time and would like to be around more people, develop repartees, laugh, repeat what we thought was funny on TV. I am bored. And the job seems easy.*

I struggle in the emptiness in my head, aware that as I make these thoughts, my interviewers are watching my immobile face, my downcast eyes, both of them uncomfortable now. How ignorant they are of the true complexity of their question! Finally, I breathe.

"I need something with which to justify my existence. I'm still trapped in the Puritan, pre-American ideal of work ethic as a means to emulate God, who made the world in six days. I am lonely a great deal of the time and would like to be around more people, develop repartees, laugh, repeat what we thought was funny on TV. I am bored. And the job seems easy."

\#

As I take a stool at the bar I realize I've forgotten my plastic bag in the conference room, under the table. I should have left it with the receptionist. I wipe my palms on my pants as panic begins to creep along my scalp. Again, I catalog my possessions — keys, pens, address book, cell phone. It all seems unnecessary.

The bartender pulls two dripping glasses out of the rinse water, setting them upside down on a towel pad underneath the bar. "What would you like?" she says, wiping her hands on a dishtowel hanging from the sink.

"Uh," I say, looking wildly at the bottles along the mirrors behind the bar, hoping my eyes will land on something I can say.

"We have beer," she says.

"Beer," I say, relieved. "Anything. The cheapest."

She sets a bottle of Miller Light on a paper coaster in front of me. The first drink I gulp down more than I intend, and burp into my fist.

From my seat I look out from the dimness to the path of sunlight made by the open door. Lehua would get a laugh from this one. All my failures amuse her — but her amusement makes more damn sense than me being upset about it. The past fifteen years, one unbroken series of failures.

I take a drink and wave my hand for another. I won't fail her, though. No matter what Shaun Francisco thinks. I will pay for them and protect them, defend them from all the shit in the world.

Executioner in the Lunchroom

A week after I started at my new job, Caroline—the woman who'd held the position before me—was fired. "Let go" was how my supervisor put it, "because things weren't working out." Caroline had trained me the first couple of days and, after she was sure I had things figured out on my own, moved to the Central Business Office downtown—to a higher position, or so I had thought. She worked two days at the Central Business Office and that was it. I probably would have never learned about her termination if, after an idle period when I had been reading about Luxembourg on Wikipedia, I hadn't wandered into Hannah's office with an apple muffin I'd taken from the lunchroom.

"So how's Caroline doing in her new digs?" I asked.

"Caroline's been let go," Hannah said, clicking cells away from a multi-colored Excel spreadsheet.

"Really?"

"Yep," Hannah said. "Things weren't really working out. Did you get the chance to update the email contact list?"

Whew, I said—inwardly, of course—as I turned around. I went back to my desk and considered what I'd heard, growing mildly outraged by the second. The whole thing was too calculated, too callously strategic. Caroline had been removed from the support system of her office coworkers—Danielle, Linda, Abbey and Anne-Marie—placed in an isolated, alien environment, then abruptly "let go." And to make matters worse, she was fired when she presumed she was being promoted.

First came the relief of "at least it's her, and not me," then the guilt of "was I chosen to replace her?" and finally the chilling conclusion of "it could just have easily—it can just as easily—be me." I looked at my coworkers—her coworkers—with a new suspicion. What did they know? What had been said? I didn't expect any of my new peers to tell me why Caroline had been fired, but I knew that, if I wanted to avoid the same destiny, I had to discover what she did wrong. And do the opposite.

To the under-the-breath office whisperings which, at first, I thought wouldn't concern me, I turned a new ear, stretching my neck ostrich-like so my head partially crested the top of my cubicle wall. But with the fundamentally bad acoustics in an office, along with the constant air conditioning and all the computers on at once and the sink intermittently screaming in the lunchroom contrapuntal to the printer spluttering out page after page in poisonous spite, I barely caught any of the gossip, just the usual fragments of baby birthdays and engagement rings. In all, I only heard Caroline's name mentioned once — and in conjunction with the name, a rush of sibilant letters out of which I hungered for words, reasons. It sounded like "Executive Officer."

That she made, through a clumsy series of deceptions and back-stabbings, a play for the position of Executive Officer before she was exposed was unlikely, considering how far down in the company's hierarchy she (and I) was. Did she say something offensive in confidence to a coworker about the Executive Officer? Or was the situation steeped in more carnal intrigue — an affair, an exchange of illicit emails, a cunning blackmail scheme by one of the staff? Who was this Executive Officer? Was it even an actual title?

In an attempt to have my ears present everywhere at once, I often took pointless walks to the lunchroom, past the desks of my colleagues engaged in conversations low in volume. I'd wash my hands, drink glasses of water, open and close the refrigerator. These covert reconnoitering operations were just as fruitless, and with a month wasted I had only the threat, becoming less vague every day, of being fired as Caroline was fired. The only way to save myself, I ceaselessly repeated, was to not do as she did.

On one of these Friday journeys to the lunchroom I was held back at the entrance, my whistle stopped mid-time, hands frozen in my pockets. A man with a prominent slouch leaned over the long table, sitting opposite the counter with the microwave and the coffee machine. The man, tall and bony, had blatantly disregarded the business-casual rule of the office: he wore no pleated slacks, no patent leather shoes, no Reyn Spooner faded inside-out Aloha shirt. Instead, the pale white skin of his thin arms and legs was exposed by a gray t-shirt and thigh-high gym shorts, low-top Chuck Taylors on his feet. While his outfit struck me as bizarre, what I found truly disturbing was the black canvas sack over his head, the upper left corner hanging at a droop. He cradled a styrofoam cup of milky coffee in long fingers. In sudden terror, I spun on the heel of my Hush Puppies and scrambled back to my desk.

I wasn't about to mention what I'd seen to anyone. In the thin, climate-controlled air of the office, overheard words can take on an uncomfortable weight they wouldn't normally take on in the house, say, or on the basketball court, where exclamations like "Damn!" and "Shit!" burst out regularly and fade away. In the office, one must be careful in everything one says; for every five words overheard by a coworker, a hundred conjectures will be disseminated. The last thing I would ask Abbey or Anne-Marie was who the hell was wearing an executioner's hood in the lunchroom. For all I knew, it could have been anyone's brother or son, their deformity hidden, come to visit. I'd once seen a woman exit a car with a similar black cloth over her face at the Makiki trailhead. Leprosy? Well, I didn't ask her.

And more rationally, I didn't want to reward what could have been the flash of a hallucination, an exaggerated daydream, with the consideration that it might have been real.

When it was clear my coworkers, perhaps not even consciously, but with the instinctual tendency to protect their own, closed ranks and stopped talking about the Caroline incident altogether, I went to the collection of three-ring binders in a shelf along the wall of our office. Caroline had kept meticulous records of her long association with the organization. She'd organized her correspondence in the binders, emails with clients and supervisors and coworkers mostly concerning meetings, upcoming conferences and assorted memos she'd drawn up about in-service trainings, policy changes, and welcome luncheons. I was sure that, in these binders, I would find the documentation I needed, the proof of Caroline's poor performance that led directly to her termination.

Beginning from the earliest pages, just after Caroline had apparently received her college degree and accepted the position, I saw that, despite some lapses of formality (using the collective "you folks" instead of the objective "you," or "see ya" instead of "Sincerely" as an exit tag) the majority of Caroline's emails were friendly, professional, and grammatically correct. There was an occasional misspelling, but these errors were so sporadic they were probably typos, rather than based in a central wrongness. Going further into the emails I saw how Caroline's style of business correspondence evolved (she began to favor "Aloha" as a greeting and "Mahalo" as her farewell) and her notes, memos and announcements became less wordy, more concise, more strictly informational, more cordial.

At the same time, her email relationships with the recipients of the daily letters grew deeper and more complex. "I heard about your mother and I wanted to extend my sympathies" one letter stated, "by the way." "I know what it's like to lose a loved one so close." Another letter requested the recipient to "drop by the office some time—this Friday would be best—we're ordering pizza!" And another: "Are you feeling better? I hope so. The last time I had the flu I was out of commission for nearly a month." What I slowly began to understand was that I, with an atavistic aversion to mixing with my coworkers under casual circumstances, would never develop the kind of rapport with others in the organization that Caroline had established.

Nowhere did I find evidence of Caroline not fulfilling some task, of her being rude or condescending to a colleague, or of being generally disorganized—all of her emails, even, were arranged first by the name of correspondent in tabs in the binder, then chronologically by date. Her system was flawless. As an administrative assistant hired specifically for her organizational skills, she was far more advanced than I could ever be, with a head for even the most peripheral matters like office birthdays, wedding anniversary dates, and funerals.

So why was she fired?

And would they get rid of me, too?

No, I was not going to let them let me go. Because of a long series of missteps throughout my life, I was now working at a job for which I had only minimal qualifications and getting paid well under what many would consider appropriate for one of my education. But I needed the income—there were loans to pay back, rent, the rising price of gasoline, food, beer, drugs, karaoke, and what-not. If I lost this, my last chance to fit into the wage-driven economic system I'd previously held in contempt, I was surely headed to the debtor's prison before the inevitable pauper's grave. And I hadn't yet become so desperate as to join that doomed, happy-go-lucky group.

Thus threatened—not with a direct sentence or penalty, but with the fear that it all could collapse on me at any moment—everything in the office took on a sinister, hostile characteristic. When I opened the upper cabinet above my desk, instead of a staple remover I saw the open jaws of a fanged serpent, its invisible coils wrapped around the two-hole punch. Pencils in a coffee mug were the wooden stakes Kurtz had decorated with severed heads. When I saw a new stapler had been placed on my desk by a (kind? insidious? thoughtful? forgetful?) coworker, I disassembled it completely, searching for the miniature camera or microphone bug.

I was running for my life. The only way, I felt, I could postpone my termination (would it be today? the next?) was to develop office processes only comprehended by me. In this way I would become invaluable. Although I wanted to make it perfectly clear how industrious, how busy I always was—even making false statements about completing tasks I hadn't been given—I couldn't let anyone know how I did these things.

For instance, I could make myself appear productive by overhauling the filing cabinet to which I had jurisdiction. While they all thought I was putting the documents in better order, I instead established a filing system based upon the Russian alphabet. There were enough correspondences between the English and Russian alphabets that, at first glance, the files would seem conventionally arranged; however, after the third letter my Russian system was unintelligible and frustrating.

"Where's that reimbursement form for Kawabata?" Hannah asked, standing puzzled over the open drawer of the cabinet. "I was sure I put it in here."

"Kawabata," I said, springing from my desk. "Coming right up." With a flourish of fingers I retrieved the paper in seconds.

"Great," Hannah said, studying the form as she walked back to her office. She turned back to me. "You have to show me what you've done with the files."

"At your service," I said, knowing I'd never tell.

I also stopped officially communicating in person or over the telephone so I could collect evidence of what exactly everyone said and when. For every task I was assigned, or favor I was asked, or idle inquiry directed to me, I now required documentation. I explicitly refused to disseminate any information that wasn't authorized with a written request.

"Hello," I remember saying at my desk once, while working out on paper a means to incorporate a number-subset into my increasingly complex files.

"Hey, it's me. Can you shoot over a schedule of—"

"Send me an email," I said.

"But I just needed—"

"So I don't forget," I said.

Another time: "Could you bring salad for Debbie's pot luck?"

"Sure, just email me with the details."

"It's the day after tomorrow. You're bringing salad."

"I'll look out for that email."

At the end of the day I went through all the emails and followed leads, constructed theories and drew conclusions. Most of them—all actually—proved to be incorrect. Although I was wrong, I had to, to be safe, know beyond a doubt that I was safe. And to know this I had to always be cautious, if not suspicious.

I also kept up-to-the-minute logs of what people said and how they behaved in a steno pad I hid under an innocuous pile of scratch paper in the bottom drawer of my desk. In order to penetrate deeper into the shadow world of Danielle, Linda, and Ann-Marie, I initiated conversations on false premises, after which I'd scribble brief synopses. Soon I was playing the part so well I didn't know if I genuinely liked these people or was simply trying to destroy them before they took me down. When someone tells you about their husband's laziness, or their kids' private school tuition, or their pet's health problems, you can't help empathy from bleeding through your fear, no matter how banal their concerns may be. After one particularly humorous bull session at Linda's desk, Ann-Marie put her hand on my arm, motherly.

"How come you never want to eat with us at lunch? You're always at your desk, all quiet and writing something."

"I know," added Danielle. "Always in that little notebook."

"Yeah, I saw that too. You writing some kind of book, or what?"

"No, no book. Sonnets, actually."

"We went to Mini Garden for lunch today," Ann-Marie said. "We got plenty. Why don't you join us?"

"Well," I said.

"Yes, join us. We have so much food."

"Join us, join us," they said, and I looked at them, conflicted.

"Sure," I said, finally. Updating the log could wait.

As a group we marched to the lunchroom, talking over one another in delight about Shrek III and the Lion King Broadway performance that was coming to Hawaii. For my own part, I was just about to add that I wasn't all that disappointed about the Transformers movie when I stopped at the entrance, the banal statement frozen in my throat.

There in his seat was the thin, sickly man in the black hood. With one hand he pulled the lower opening of his mask wide while with the other he lifted a sandwich on toast to his uncovered mouth. My coworkers went to the sink, went to the refrigerator, set out paper plates and moved among him while he ate silently.

"Come, come," they chanted, pulling out a chair for me, waving me in.

"I've got to—I've got to do something," I said lamely, turning away. I fled the office, took a seat on the stone bench outside the Central Union church a block away, and watched a series of limousines pull up to the steps as Japanese couples went inside to get married. What had I seen? When the lunch hour was over, I went back to my desk and said nothing.

Constant surveillance, along with rigid, all-encompassing documentation and the maintenance of a filing system I soon found to be incomprehensible took most of my work day. Soon I was behind in the work I'd been hired to do, so intent as I was in becoming a fixture, un-fireable, irreplaceable. I whited-out and rewrote dates on forms to meet deadlines, delegated forgotten duties to coworkers by burying memos deep in their in-boxes. Unbeknownst to them, there could be any number of assignments already late. When Hannah asked me for something I didn't have, I immediately blamed someone else for not following through.

"Where's that agenda for the meeting?" she'd demand.

"I gave it to Cyrus like days ago," I'd say—and Cyrus would look confused, and then promise to do better.

A bureaucracy is really quite easy to manipulate when everyone takes it on good faith that you'll do the job you were hired to do. Although I did little real work, I knew the requirements and objectives and how certain papers functioned and to where they were delivered so well that I could falsify paperwork at any level, providing forged signatures for contracts and agreements the signatory had "forgotten" she'd approved.

I'd become entrenched in the system, as I'd wanted—

I'd gotten so involved, and so independent of anyone else that, were they to attempt to "let me go" at any time, their entire machine would break into incongruent fragments. As long as I could maintain this illusion to myself, they would all believe.

I forgot about Caroline.

There were too many other things to consider. After three months I felt like I'd been working with the organization forever, powering the system with phony documents, with lies and the offspring of lies. No one mentioned Caroline anymore, and no one remembered she'd worked there.

"Who?"

"Caroline," the woman said to the receptionist. She pointed behind Ann-Marie to me, where I sat drawing a schematic of the levels of authority in our organization. It all went back to the Executive Officer.

"Caroline," she repeated. "She used to sit at that desk."

"No Caroline here," Ann-Marie said. The rest of them shook their heads. I looked up from my drawing for just a moment, looked at the woman, and looked away.

Friday, after I closed my cupboard, changed again the lock password on my PC before powering it down, and set my ball point pen at a 43 degree angle on my desk (according to a protractor I'd taken from one of the designers in graphics) to test whether anyone went through my things while I was gone for the weekend, the dramatic, almost ecstatic, understanding that it would all end soon fell onto my shoulders like hammers, vibrating out of my fingertips in tingling static electricity. Despite what the counterfeit schedules said, or what was written on the request to purchase forms, or who put what into the time sheets, and no matter whose signatures those senseless scrawls for verification and authorization might look like, it would all lead back to me. If only one person bothered to double-check what was apparent, they would see that what was apparent represented a projection only, a non-existence.

And I could hardly keep it up much longer. There was the brief notion that I could perhaps go back, shred some particularly incriminating evidence, repair the damage I'd done to my integrity, my reputation, and my professional career — and, at this point, most likely the organization — but the machine's now fundamental dependence on me to run properly, no matter how flimsy the pretext and how corrupt the fuel, would have been lost. I would have been as unnecessary as Caroline.

Besides, there wasn't enough time to fix anything. How could I go back? Never enough time. I now shoved papers into file folders willy-nilly, dropped faxes directly into the garbage can. But my professional façade hadn't yet cracked — even though the dread of the inevitable revelation had infected every thought with stomach-churning fear, I issued a hearty "have a nice weekend" to the coworkers whom, engaged as they were in legitimate work at their desks, looked up at me and smiled and waved.

On Sunday I wandered the city with a pocket radio, down the broad one-way streets of King and Beretania, past restaurants I'd never eat in and boutiques from which I'd never buy anything. While talk radio belabored Fatah, Hamas, Iraq and Afghanistan, and the roads rumbled and roared with wheezy buses and squealing mopeds, I could not but contemplate my trouble and misery, half-heartedly attempting plans to get out of the mess. In the late afternoon the rain came and tires hissed and spit against the slick asphalt. Wet, I walked into the uncomfortable air-conditioned chill of the Goodwill store, clothes in bright, out-of-date hues hanging all around me, each garment smelling of old person's skin. I felt tired. I felt weak.

With a ten-dollar bill in my pocket — and too sad to use it to get drunk — I paid for a matinee show at the Academy of Arts, where they played Clint Eastwood's Bird. The film did nothing to pull me out of my self-inflicted funk; if anything, it reinforced the certainty that the monster I'd built to protect me would ultimately dismember and decapitate me. The music in the film was nice, though, and for a few minutes while the film ran and the sound came through the speakers I imagined I was a note on the saxophone, expelled into the world to be beautiful for a splendid moment before I was set free.

I left the show when it was dark outside, with mists swirling around the street lamp bulbs after another light shower. With my radio off I went towards my apartment listening to the rubbery whisperings of wheels on the wet road. Under the University Avenue overpass the white doves tucked their necks deep into their feathers for the night. At the Atherton YMCA I crossed the avenue and looked into the window. Inside, silhouettes in profile danced couples to the big band music I'd heard on the sidewalk. I thought, what is this place?

I'd gone to the YMCA several Sundays in a row before I'd landed a job with the organization, but since I'd started working, I'd been too busy plotting, too busy covering up. Without being exposed to swing music in my childhood, I felt its rhythms were somehow imprinted on my genetic code, an evolutionary holdover from the sacred mating rituals of my grandparents. Those forgotten months before I began working I'd walk in nonchalantly, take a chair along the wall, and pretend not to study anyone in the dimness. Suddenly, in the middle of a song, I'd stand up and walk over to two girls invariably sitting together, talking close and under the music, and ask the less pretty one for a dance. After a few songs, after I dipped her and twirled her and both of us sweating and laughing, the discretion would fall away, the rest of the evening simple and nice.

As I watched those figures that night — they seemed cut from dark cloth, waving through the window — I couldn't imagine joining them, losing myself in the low lights and sentimental music. It wasn't that I only had three dollars left and didn't know how much longer I'd have an income. I felt that, in the span of a few months, I wasn't the same person of Sundays long ago; I wasn't a dancer and an appreciator of simpler times. I had become antithesis to who I'd been. What I was seeing was not real and the shadows moving before me, lifelike as they seemed through the glass, were shadows only.

"Jonah," someone called from behind. Though it didn't sound like my own name, I turned, wondering with whom I'd been confused.

A young woman approached slowly from under a bright curtain of street light and then into the darkness of the night in which I stood. That she was a head shorter than me was all I could discern until she stood right in front of me, looking up through long hair parted down the middle.

"Jonah," she repeated.

"You mean me?" I said.

"Yes, Jonah. It's me, Caroline."

"Caroline—"

"Caroline, Caroline," she said, and shook out her head as if trying to scrub away a bad picture that had developed on top of her brain. "I worked with you. I had your job."

"Caroline," I said, trying to think back. A black, foggy cavern seemed to have been installed in the space reserved for memories I'd had before I started to work for the organization. "Caroline," I said again, now feeling the easy familiarity of her name over my tongue, through my lips. "Did we date?"

"No—just try to remember."

"Caroline—you were fired!" But this couldn't have been the Caroline I knew. Not only did she seem happier, healthier, her skin almost glowing in the darkness—this was a different person.

"Let go," she said, correcting me.

"Right," I said.

"So I take it you're still there? How is it going?"

"Great," I said, and she nodded skeptically. "Caroline, tell me, please. Please. Why were you let go?"

"Haven't you figured it out yet?"

"Figured what out?"

"Look at the records, Jonah. Look at the emails."

"I've looked at them," I said. "They don't show anything. Except that maybe you were pretty good at your job."

"It seems that way, doesn't it?" she said. She looked down.

"But things look like they're a lot better for you now," I said, still not sure if she and I were thinking of the same Caroline.

"Read the logs again, Jonah," she said. "It's all in the records. And it's not just my story, it's yours, too." She gripped my arm and walked past me in to the YMCA. One of the girls I could have danced with on any number of nights and I'd never have known it.

I went to work early on Monday, turned on my desk lamp and hunched down low over the binder with Caroline's records so my head wouldn't be seen over the partitions of my cubicle. Page by page, memo by memo, everything was the same as I'd originally read it, the some content with the same greetings and pleasantries. I flipped through the plastic protected papers frantically, nearly ripping them out of the rings from their three-punch holes, until I caught the single thing I'd missed, imprinted at the top of an older document.

Where Caroline's name was once written on an otherwise inconsequential address line from a document sent years before, was now the name Jonah; Jonah, the name I'd failed to recognize. Although it felt like I'd been with the organization longer than three months, I was sure the dates on the emails couldn't be correct. I'd never sent—but there was the message in the same business-casual diction I employed for all-around office correspondence. Turning back on the pages I saw that, printed at the top of each was Jonah and Jonah and Jonah, no mention of any Caroline. Had she ever worked here? Jonah—why did it sound so different coming from my coworkers' mouths, why so foreign to my own ears?

No, the name read Jonah, but it was Caroline. Or rather, it was always, and always would be, Caroline, just as it always was and would be Jonah. The names were insignificant; it was always the work.

Caroline, or at least the part of her that had worked diligently at her position for five years, whose greater day was spent filing, typing, and organizing—supporting an organization of mysterious hierarchy and arbitrary regulations—Caroline hadn't gone anywhere. That none of us could remember her name, or what she had looked like, or that she had been at this desk only a few months ago was proof that her presence had metamorphosed—she'd been absorbed into the organization. Caroline and her five years were now essential to, inseparable from—the same as—the physical make up of a larger entity. Her current state of being was so dissimilar from the old form that no one needed to recall her name or her appearance. The past Caroline went on continuing the same work she'd always done. She was still here, as all the others before were still here, and I was here temporarily; the vessel that would carry on the interminable task, to make manifest the unachieved visions of the souls who had failed before me.

I went through the book quickly now, my own name blurring from the address lines.

"Jonah," someone said from behind.

Pushing myself away from my desk, I swiveled in my rolling chair and looked up at Hannah. "The Executive Officer would like to meet with you."

"Sure," I said. I closed the binder and took up my favorite office-issued pen.

"Leave the pen," Hannah said.

I passed my coworkers and no one wasted the effort to glance up at me; Anne-Marie even went so far as to shove her way past me to the postage machine without even an "excuse me." Perhaps I'd become insubstantial. Perhaps, in their eyes, I'd already disappeared. I followed Hannah down a series of hallways before she threw open the door to an office on the corner of a lower floor, isolated from all the activity of the organization.

All the bosses, from every level, sat in a row in front of me — Hannah took the last open seat — and I stood behind the single chair facing them. In front of each of my superiors was a sheaf of incriminating papers, not only of what I'd done, but the illicit acts committed by those in my position years — generations — before. They said nothing, waiting for me to speak first.

And behind them, standing over their shoulders in his black hood and gym gear, was the man I'd come to know as the Executioner. Afraid — but also relieved, as is the prisoner of war when finally set against the wall and blindfolded — I found no lies, no excuses at my disposal. My efforts to become indispensable to the organization were all irrelevant. After a few moments staring at me while I bit my lips, the executioner silently slid the black cloth from his face.

I saw nothing extraordinary in his features — like mine, his face was plain, nothing you'd remember from a crowded bus or the wide promenade of a shopping center. But in his now uncovered eyes was the pity and sympathy I'd only read about in the tales of saints and religious mystics. All at once they took me in, and all at once all the wrongness fell out of me. Kind and sad, the Executioner looked at me and waited.

"I couldn't—" I began, and told them everything, no equivocations to assuage the guilt.

He didn't interrupt me or ask to clarify. He merely lay me down and stroked me with his unblinking eyes. The more I confessed, the freer I felt. I finished, looking down, and the room remained silent. When I raised my eyes to the Executioner I knew he would let me go, and that I was forgiven.

Honolulu Labyrinth Society

"When you folks were talking about labyrinths, I thought you meant the walking kind," Angie said, pulling her boss's mail from its cubbyhole along the wall. "I love labyrinths."

"Really?" I said. I threw my boss's junk mail into the trashcan at our feet. Moments earlier, Tiana had mentioned the movie *Labyrinth*, with David Bowie in his shimmering white wig and all those ugly puppets, and this struck me as coincidental because she'd no idea that I'd just bought Borges' *Labyrinths* from Jelly's. The purchase was based on a recommendation from one of David's friends, along with a compulsion to buy at least *something* before I left the store.

"How long have you loved labyrinths?" I said, leaning into the wall of mailboxes, staring Angie down. Angie went through great pains to drop into anyone's conversation, often under false pretenses. I wanted to catch her in her lie — it was at least more entertaining than going back to the desk to look over the payroll records.

"Oh Lisa, there's tons of them around town. Labyrinths all over. I go to one nearly every weekend. And the world's biggest walking maze is right on the North Shore."

I stepped closer to her. "That's funny," I said. "Because in twenty-five years I've never even heard of a single labyrinth in Honolulu."

Bernadette walked by, drying her hands with a paper towel. "Hey, you guys missed the birthday song," she said. In one smooth hook shot, she propelled the wadded paper over the rim of the waste basket. "You gonna get some cake or what?"

"Does it have wheat in it?" Angie said. She'd been on and off a gluten-free diet since time immemorial.

"Well, it's cake," Bernadette said.

"A slice wouldn't hurt, I suppose," Angie said, elbowing us both simultaneously. "I'm being so bad today." I pulled back, avoiding her conspirator's coffee-stained breath.

After lunch I stared at the collection of post cards stuck to my workstation walls with push pins, miniature prints I'd collected from the Van Gogh museum and the Honolulu Academy of Arts, pictures of mountains and bridges and rivers. Spaced unevenly apart, the postcards created a pattern, almost map-like, and in the blank spaces between the rectangles, I saw lines that could have been corridors, empty spaces formed by the edges of pictures that could have been chambers. I saw, on my wall, a maze I'd unconsciously formed to keep the banality of paperwork from drowning me in monochrome. The labyrinth had reappeared. I traveled several trails through the post cards with my eyes from one side of the wall to the other, then spun my chair to face the computer and typed "labyrinth Hawai'i" into the Google search engine.

Labyrinth. It was a weird word — the only word I knew in which the meaning couldn't be lost through repetition, like "toy boat." In fact, I found the meaning of labyrinth made manifest, intensified even, when repeated over and over. *Labyrinthlabyrinthlabyrinthlabyrinthlabyrinth*, I said under my breath while the search results loaded on my screen. A series of verbal twists and turns displaying an end indistinguishable from the beginning.

I wanted to verify Angie's statement about labyrinths supposedly all over our fair city. The first page of internet entries was devoted to the Dole corn maze on the North Shore. A service called the "World Labyrinth Finder" sent me right back to the Dole Plantation maze after I clicked "Hawai'i" on its menu bar. I'd been to the maze once with Allan, on our third date, and I'd paid more attention to making out in the corners than minding the path.

This wouldn't have been the first time I'd caught Angie being untruthful. She told me once the cafeteria was serving hamburger steak when in reality, it was serving egg foo young. She told me she enjoyed the movie *Open Range*, even going so far as to compel me to rent it that night, and the very next day I heard her trashing the plot and the characters to Tiana. She said she avoided gluten and she ate cookies in secret at her desk. Her lies, though, weren't devious. They weren't exactly meant to mislead or offend. She simply didn't have the ability to be honest.

I found the labyrinths of which Angie might have spoken farther down on the list. First there was the meditation labyrinth at St. Andrew's cathedral — intended, as the traveler navigated its curves, for silent contemplation of man's relationship to God. An illustration of the labyrinth at St. Clement's (also of the meditation variety) displayed a symmetrical series of paths forming a muted four-leaf clover. I wrote down the addresses of these churches and continued to scroll down through duplicate sites and other ads for the World's Largest Maze.

I found the entry for "Honolulu Labyrinth Society" supplemented with no abbreviated descriptor halfway down the third page, when I had decided to close the search and, after casually walking to Angie's workstation, ask what the hell she meant by "labyrinths all over Honolulu." Depicted on the introductory window was the screen-sized outline of a bull's head, the flat space between the horns overlaid with the name of the organization. At the bottom, underlined, was the simple invitation to "enter."

A second later I was looking at the digitized newsprint of the *Honolulu Star-Advertiser*. The search engine had closed off my option to return to the site, so I idly skimmed through the linked article: a story of a seventy year old man afflicted with Alzheimer's who'd gone missing a few years ago. Near the bottom I found a hyperlink embedded in the word "You" from "*You don't know if they even understand the outside world anymore.*" This took me to a second newspaper article, this one from the old *Star-Bulletin*, concerning the unknown whereabouts of a sixteen-year-old girl. "Will," from "*She will find her way back — I know it*" led to an article from the *Weekly* about the lost body of a surfer, presumably eaten by a shark and "Not," from *"I'm not sure if he often went out alone"* went back to the *Star-Advertiser* about a runaway child. The last link, "Escape," took me to a black page in which an address, with no name or phone number, was printed in white text.

"You – will – not – escape," I said, ladling David another helping of the Zippy's-bought chili with which he had avoided his turn in the cooking rotation. We usually made dinner together Tuesdays and Thursdays at my apartment. David lived in a house with three other roommates and their shower drain had been clogged for months with something tenacious and evil. "That's pretty creepy, right?"

"I wouldn't say creepy," David mumbled through a mouthful of rice. "More like cheesy."

"But who would go through the trouble to make a website like that? With the articles and the lost people? Have you ever heard of the Honolulu Labyrinth Society?"

David stood up from the table and took another of my bottles of Perrier from the refrigerator.

"You better replace that," I said.

"Relax," he said. "I'm going to Costco tomorrow. I'll buy you a whole case."

"Yeah, so you can drink them all," I said.

"You know, this Honolulu Labyrinth whatever

probably doesn't even exist. Just a dumb gag made up by a loser with too much time on his hands. Why have these people never been covered by the TV or the newspaper? No one has ever heard about it? Someone would have publicized this thing."

"Don't you think it's mysterious?" I said, sliding my hand over the hairs of his forearm as he sat back down.

"That's the difference between us," he said. "What you think is mysterious I think is bad joke. I guess that's why we make such a great team."

"But you'll come with me, right? To see the labyrinths Sunday."

"Aren't we living in a labyrinth? Aren't the streets of Honolulu essentially a labyrinth?"

I drew my hand away. I'd had the suspicion for some time that David would have preferred I discard any interests not coinciding with his own, that it would be better if we merged our similar interests and I channeled the whole wad to him, a throbbing umbilical cord through which he could gain sustenance for his perfect life.

"A man says he can escape from any labyrinth in the world," David continued. "So this guy takes him up on his bet, blindfolds him, and sets him dead center in the Sahara desert. Bam, there's your labyrinth."

"All right, so everything's a labyrinth," I said. "Are you coming with me or what?"

"Everything's a labyrinth—and it's not," he replied, smug. "Can't do it. Softball at Kanewai Park. Thought you wanted to come with me."

"But I'm going to see those labyrinths, honey," I said. Going to David's softball games: I shuddered as I suppressed a yawn on behalf of the universe.

Saturday I called Renee, a friend once prettier than me who had, through an unfortunate haircut and more than twenty pounds, made herself comfortable on the less-attractive side of adult womanhood by way of cheese cakes, ice creams, plate lunches and flavored coffee drinks. While I grew my hair out and went jogging three times a week, Renee developed her body to better withstand another ice age, accumulating, along the way, the white gold rings and bracelets that would inevitably accompany her in her sarcophagus. But she still had an enthusiasm for adventure, most of which was reserved for popular fiction along the lines of the Knights Templar, Apocalypse conspiracy theories, and anything related to the imagery of the *The Da Vinci Code*. No more skinny-dipping with mainland boys for her, no driving through the Wilson tunnel on acid, no growing pot in the closet. She now read bad novels and went to restaurants with her boyfriend.

"I can't do anything today," she said. Over the receiver I heard Iron Maiden scream through speakers, the music she used to complement her reading. "Jonathan and I are going to Buca's after the movie."

That goddamn Ward Complex, I thought. The whole place was too good to be true, with its specialty shops and its Dave and Buster's. *May the Lord strike it down.*

"Well, maybe Johnny would want to come," I began.

"Labyrinths aren't his thing."

I was relieved. Johnny had broken Renee's heart two years ago. When everyone thought they'd be married he left her after a long, secret affair with a second cousin who lived in Hilo. No one suspected because they were family. Six months later, acting with what must have been a benevolent sense of grace, he came back to save Renee from what he was sure would be life-long despair. Weak as she was, she took him. He'd snuck back into all of our lives so skillfully that we all nearly forgot he'd been gone, and what for. Everyone considered him a good looking guy but, because of some freak chemistry, Johnny left me cold. I thought he was handsome enough, but not *desirable*. It must have been the kind of thing John Lennon thought when he heard "Yesterday" for the first time.

"But tomorrow," I said, over the phone to Renee. "Tomorrow you're free, right? You can come with me."

"I guess so," she said. "Shall we meet for breakfast first?"

By eleven the next morning I'd almost lost all patience. Not because I was all that eager to get to the labyrinths right away—the websites had written that the church labyrinths wouldn't be open to the public until after the morning services—but because I'd been sitting in a floral print booth at the Mapunapuna Bob's Big Boy for an hour and a half, listening to complaint-saturated tales of Johnny's misdeeds while Renee ordered refill after refill of pancakes. I'd ordered the saimin and now watched figures move across the sunny window to the entrance of the restaurant. Paying for Renee's breakfast and giving her a ride from Pearl City was part of our deal, so she'd come with me.

"And they're drunk until five in the morning—the sun's almost up already—listening to that stupid stereo. Cops came twice. Roy got wasted on Maker's Mark. You should have seen the bathroom, Lisa. Chips and salsa. The chunks—"

"Stop right there," I said, not dying to relive a memory of vomit, especially one I hadn't experienced myself.

"So how are you?" Renee said. "How is everything, really?"

I shrugged, then sipped at my water and let the ice melt between my teeth. "You know," I said finally. "There's work—I can make enough money to get from one day to the next. And David. I don't know, maybe we should just get married or something."

"And these labyrinths you're so hot over?"

"This is just because I'm bored. A labyrinth's as good a metaphor for life as any."

"Anything can be a metaphor for life."

"Anything can be a metaphor, and can't," I replied, feeling a bit queasy for robbing David of his smartass response.

I pulled into the lot at St. Andrew's cathedral while Renee opened the folded the list of addresses I'd copied at work. "The first of the so-called 'Meditation Labyrinths,'" I said. The sky through my rolled-up window was a bright hot blue against which the downtown towers crowded next to one another looked like a gray mountain range with the green all sucked away.

"What's this last address?" Renee said. "Looks like somewhere in Manoa."

"The Honolulu Labyrinth Society," I said. "They have this really silly website. Have you ever heard of them?"

"Nope."

We got out of the car.

We'd found the labyrinth by asking a man in a white shirt tucked into dirty brown slacks who had been walking diagonally across one of the lawns to Queen Street, a tied plastic bag hanging from one of his arms.

"Excuse me," I said, stepping off the paved walkway to catch him. "Can you—"

He turned abruptly as if I'd meant to accuse him of a crime he wasn't sure he committed. The plastic bag swung round and rocked at his hips.

"What do you want?" he said, his voice rising high. His eyes were shrunken beads behind thick panes of rectangular glass.

"We're just looking for the labyrinth," Renee said, coming up behind me. "Do you know where it is?"

"The labyrinth."

"That's right," I said.

"It's over there," he said, waving the plastic bag toward the church's auditorium. "But it's not really a labyrinth."

"It's not a labyrinth?"

"It's a labyrinth, but it's not a really a labyrinth."

"I don't know what you mean," Renee said.

"I mean," he said, his voice going high again. His plastic bag began wavering near his knees and I could foresee his impatience shortly becoming blind and violent rage. "I mean that there is a labyrinth but it's not really a labyrinth."

"So that's what he meant," Renee said later, as we stood looking at a two-dimensional drawing on the wall at St. Andrew's. "How were we supposed to know?" The labyrinth at St. Andrew's, we learned, was not something you went into; rather, it was something you stood before and stared at. Instead of being housed beyond a circular portal in the depths of the stone church, and lit from without by the multicolored glass depiction of Christ and his glory, the labyrinth we sought was a drawing on a concrete wall outdoors, near the rear entrance of the church's auditorium where the Hawai'i Theatre for Youth staged plays. Only a picture, just as a postcard of Diamond Head is Diamond Head and isn't. As large as a human body, the likeness of the labyrinth on the wall was in the shape of a human face, the features of which were delineated by corridors and turns. Not any particular face, not Jesus' or Iz's or John F. Kennedy's. It may have been the universal face, hairless, sexless, the naked human face that all people are born and die with. For several moments — longer than I'd intended, maybe — my eyes traced the long tunnel from an opening under the ear through the cheek, around the mouth, then sloping to the lower chin before marking the opposite inner cheek. All my senses were focused on the route my eyes traveled, through halls no wider than an inch. Though my hands were at my side, I could hear the light friction of my fingertip against the concrete wall, taste the silence, smell the broken down components of everything in the air, the stone, the gas exhaust, the grass, Renee's shampoo. And when she spoke, I felt as though I'd been pulled from the bottom of an ocean, dead, pulled unwillingly to the violent broken-up surface, to the cold light and struggle and misery.

"It's not a labyrinth," Renee said. "It's just a representation of one."

"But what does a labyrinth itself represent?" I asked.

"I don't know. Isn't a labyrinth in itself just a labyrinth?"

"Maybe," I said, and shrugged. "Well, I guess we can go see the others."

We pulled into an empty parking lot at St. Clement's after Renee had bought a coffee-esque shake at the Sure Shot Café. A wide wraparound porch surrounded the main church building, a simple wooden rectangle with several glass doors. Under the shade of the awning we stood and looked through the glass at the desolate pews, the podium in front, the large white crucifix, the flower arrangements and the hymnals, but we saw nothing indicating a labyrinth.

Behind the church a long corridor ran along the back

wall. Its floor was laid in concrete panels and fenced in from the yard by ivy-entwined black chain links, and led to a white door upon which the words "Prayer Room" had been painted in script. "Maybe it's down here," Renee said, and I followed her down the declining walkway that must have, I thought, led to a subterranean chamber. It seemed likely that a labyrinth would be built inside and underground since, especially in this city, there was so little space to be afforded to an enterprise as questionably necessary as a walking labyrinth. But the door to the "Prayer Room" was locked, a rusty affair I could have broken down with a kick.

"Damn," I said.

"Watch your mouth," Renee said.

"And there's no one to open the door for us," I said. "You know, maybe it's not even

down there. Maybe it's somewhere else."

We walked around the premises looking for any kind of entrance, opening the latch on a gate that separated the elementary school buildings from the church. Short water fountains, stunted playground equipment, and stairwells decorated with turtles and other less obvious smiling sea creatures. Educational toys and school supplies lay on shelves near the windows of classrooms, and brooms and dry mops stood propped in corners. Every turn took us to the limits of the grounds, a tall chain link fence marking property ownership between the church and the parking lot of the apartment building next door. One path led us to a water spigot leaking onto a bed of gravel. Another found us in front of the administrative office, its chair abandoned, the morose computer screen powered-down and unlit, papers strewn every which way across the desk. One grim fact became quickly obvious from our search—nowhere on the grounds of St. Clement's was there space enough to support a labyrinth.

"It could be that the church itself—the school and everything—that's the labyrinth," Renee said as we stood leaning on the car.

"What a ripoff," I said.

"But I thought you said everything was a labyrinth."

"It's not what they portrayed on their website. There was supposed to be a walking labyrinth, one-third of a mile, in the shape of some symmetrical flower-petal thing. You can't just call your yard a labyrinth. It's misleading."

"Well, anyways—wait, look!"

"Where?"

"On the ground. The whole parking lot!"

For one strange moment my eye went above my head, floating upwards and gazing directly below to Renee and me in the midst of a flower-petal labyrinth, its edges of white paint, the sinuous grace of its lines, interrupted by my car parked at a slant. Then my vision fell back into me and I walked along the painted shape spread out before me until I found the entrance.

"It's not what I expected but—well, here we go."

"What? You're actually going to walk this thing?"

"That's what we came for, right?"

Renee followed me through the outer rim of the first petal. I found it difficult to concentrate on the path before me, hearing only Renee's rubber slippers scraping behind. I pulled my sunglasses down over my nose. The white lines were too bright to look at for long, and the sun, in its afternoon fury, felt like warm, uncomfortable hand tightening around the back of my neck. Renee's phone rang and I turned to look at her.

"Hey. We're just looking for labyrinths. No, not looking in labyrinths, looking for them. Apparently there's a lot of them around. Why, what are you up to? What? I think so. I'll ask her. I'll call you back, okay?"

I sighed. While looking at Renee I'd stepped out of my prescribed line.

"I gotta go," Renee said. "Johnny wants me to meet up. California Pizza Kitchen."

"What, Pearlridge? I got to drive all the way back to

that side now?"

"No, he's in town. Ala Moana."

"What about the Honolulu Labyrinth Society?"

Renee looked at me. "I can wait for you to finish this labyrinth before we go."

"Let's go already then."

Driving into Manoa valley, that green land scarce of sidewalk, I felt driven to extract some kind of meaning, any kind of meaning, out of my search for a labyrinth. What was I looking for in looking for a labyrinth? What would I find inside of the labyrinth? The journey was better alone, at least. Renee had just been a distraction. And I could easily imagine David's complaints if he'd come along, how stupid he'd think it was, I was, how much force he'd put into convincing me to do something else, something he wanted to do.

As usual, gray threadbare clouds sidled over the mountain ridges in the distance. I couldn't gauge how soon it would rain. As University Avenue converged into Oahu Road, I understood I was entering a new world, darker and more lush.

I found the Honolulu Labyrinth Society down a narrow road farther up near the mountains, a solitary property at a dead end. A sign in yellow lettering on brown wood hung from a post in front of a square, one-storied building with screened windows and a front door slightly open. After I made sure there were no No Parking signs along the roadside I stopped my car at the cul-de-sac and walked over the squishing, damp lawn to the lonely building.

Knocking once on the thin, shuddering screen door, I turned off the stoop to look up at the houses nestled in greenery on the mountainside above me, flat patches of brown and white and brick red between clusters of treetops. When no one answered, I pulled the door towards me and called inside—surprisingly, and somewhat unnervingly, a phlegmy voice answered and asked me to please come in. I kicked my slippers off at the door step and entered a living room more spacious than it should have been, cavernous almost, twice as deep as it gave the impression of being when viewed from the outside.

A miniature old man sat drowning in the plush of an overstuffed easy chair. Apparently he'd been gazing at nothing before I'd come in, no television on, no radio playing, no cell phone in his hand, no book open on his lap. For a place supposedly representing a labyrinth, this great room was quite uncomplicated. Spaced out over the thick green carpet was the easy chair, a wooden rocker at rest in its grooves, and a pile of faded, but still firm, pillows piled in a corner. Shelves with the spines of new books upright lined each of the four walls, the gaps between the tomes patterned as if by design, like roll music for a player piano. The outstanding feature was the arrangement of portraits high on one wall over a bookshelf, enlarged and framed black and white photographs of uniform size randomly hanging from the white wall, some set far apart, others crowded together. Near the ceiling one of the portraits, apparently the victim of the daily morning sun blasting through the window, had become so washed out as to match the white paint of the wall.

"I thought this was the labyrinth society," I said.

"It was," the old man wheezed, waving at the portraits with a thin arm. "Before all of them —"

He struggled to pull himself into an erect sitting position in the capacious chair. The old man's jeans were worn at the knees, but clean and faded to an almost bright light-blue. Through the two top open buttons of a yellowing white shirt I saw a heavy, Masonic-looking symbol dangling from his neck on a golden cord. "I'm the only one left."

"So there's no more labyrinth, then," I said, resigned at once to turn back to my car, to integrate myself back into David's universe and the arbitrary practices of work and life. It's always been my bad luck to get interested in something already long gone.

"The labyrinth's still there, if you want to see it," the

old man said. For a moment, he tried to get up—maybe he wanted to show me—but then slid farther into the recesses of his easy chair, the effort too taxing.

"A labyrinth? Really?"

"Hedge, if that suits you," the man replied. "I still tend to it twice a week."

"But the labyrinth society," I said.

"Just you and me, kid."

"So—what for?"

"For them. For all of us. For you, especially."

"Right," I said, doing my best impersonation of someone humoring someone else. "How much does it cost?"

"It's free," he said. "In a sense."

"And what's that supposed to mean?"

"It means it doesn't cost any money. Go on, go look at it. You'll see it round the back. Spend the rest of the day there, if you like."

"Well—thanks," I said. Once outside I saw the tall hedges the small man had kept trimmed to square corners, and was surprised I hadn't spotted them before I'd gone inside the house. An interruption in the wall of gleaming green leaves indicated the open entrance. Far beyond, just before I stepped past the first row of hedges, I saw the mountain ridges receding under wind-flowing swaths of mists. The formerly bright day had aged into a grim afternoon.

I looked back at my car, still worried about the hazards of parking on these uninhabited Manoa side streets — as a rule, the elderly residents, who had nothing better to do, would tow a car away for the sheer pleasure of it. When I faced forward I nearly collided with a figure emerging from the labyrinth, whose footsteps and crackling plastic bag I hadn't heard until he was upon me. The man from St. Andrew's stopped, the pinpoints of his eyes attempting to break through the thick lenses of his glasses to recognize me from only a few hours earlier. I smelled the exact kind of place where he must have slept the previous night. I smelled the whole city, the whole world and its clashing scents raging around his person.

"You," I said, startled.

"You," he said. I wasn't sure if he was mimicking my reaction or was surprised as me. He went past me to the road. "It's a real labyrinth," he called out, not turning back, and I waited until he cleared the corner of the dead-end street before I went in.

The hedges cut off all view of the outside except for the omnipresent mountain ridges swimming in gray moisture and the dome of the darkening sky above me. The labyrinth had been well tended, each passageway of seemingly equal width carpeted in mown grass, not a single rough bush crowding in along the walking path. And it was a real labyrinth, not a maze—my trail towards the end was laid out before me with no choice but forward, giving no opportunity to blaze my way through twists and turns. I simply followed.

Going deeper, I realized the walls I'd seen from outside the labyrinth belied its interior dimensions. Turn after successive turn formed an increasingly complex pattern I could not grasp, especially since I was in the middle of it. I made a note to ask the old man in the house for an aerial of the labyrinth when I came out. This thought led to other questions. Who made the Honolulu Labyrinth Society website? That prune? And why had it been portrayed as so sinister? The turns, not conventional right angles—which made me think the labyrinth was neither square nor rectangular in shape—flowed easily into one another, unadorned except for the occasional hibiscus that had broken through the thick leaves of the hedge.

The repetition of walking a short distance before turning on my heel down another corridor of leaves and branches grew tiresome. The ambition and adrenalin that had agitated me into action earlier began to dissipate. Somewhere near what might have been the middle of the labyrinth, I wanted out. The hedge walls that had seemed so evenly spaced at the beginning were now too close, too unnecessarily towering. I turned around, wondering if it would be faster to follow my path back out. But then I thought of David, and what I would have to tell him about my failure, and I set my foot forward and made the next turn deeper into the labyrinth.

And just as I cleared another hedge, I saw David walking towards me. Shocked, I said nothing until I reached out and shoved him on the chest.

"David?"

"Oh. Hey Squirt."

"David, what are you doing here? Did you follow me or something?"

"What am I doing here. That's a good question. I'm just walking, I suppose." He spread his arms, gesturing to our surroundings. "Walking through the labyrinth."

"Well—duh," I said. "But you said you had softball. I thought you thought this was all stupid. And how—how did you end up going the opposite way?"

"I guess I thought this was the right way." He looked at me, waiting for something.

"That's really weird," I said. "But I'm glad you came, David. We might as well finish it together." I took his hand.

"But that's not the right way," he said, pulling me

towards the way I'd come.

"Yes it is, David. Come on."

"No. The end is this way."

"But I already came that way. I want to finish it my way."

"But it's not the right way."

"Look, David, I know which way I came and which way I need to go. If you want to keep going that way, fine. I'll meet you outside."

He glared at me, his nostrils wide. Then he shrugged and began to lead me—lead *me*—down the path whence he'd come. I let go of his hand but followed, now not so glad that he'd dropped softball to catch up with me.

"How come you wanted to do this stupid labyrinth anyway?"

"If you think it's so stupid, then why the hell are you here?" I said.

Before he responded I saw the dim backs of two shapes walking ahead. "David, there's people here."

"I see them," he said.

"David, Lisa," Johnny said, turning back at us, having heard the shushed whisper of our footsteps on the grass before we'd reached him. His arm was around Renee as if he'd just been talking intimately into her ear: giving her secret orders, probably. Johnny didn't seem all that happy to see us and Renee, subdued, gave a toothless and embarrassed smile.

"Wait—did you all plan this together?" I said, looking at Renee.

"Nah, we're just moving through the labyrinth, same as you," Johnny said. "But now that we're all here, we might as well make it a group effort."

"We don't—" I stopped and stared at the three of them. Here I'd had this thing, my thing, that I'd resolved to accomplish on my own, and fucking Johnny stood in front of me like it was his idea all along. Renee glanced up at me but for some reason wouldn't hold my eye. "Fine," I said, passing the three of them to make it clear it was my journey, and that they were the usurpers. "But I thought you guys thought all this was stupid."

"How come you wanted to do this labyrinth anyway?" Johnny said from behind.

"Jesus Christ, I don't know," I said, not turning back to address him. "I just thought it was important, that's all."

"Yeah, how come," Renee said quietly.

"What, you didn't hear me? I don't know why."

"How come, Lisa?" a new voice asked—and I spun around, sure it couldn't be—but my mother, a head shorter than Renee, stood behind them, in her muumuu and brown slippers. They watched me expectantly. Angie appeared from behind a hedge and joined them at the rear.

"I don't know why," I said, but without the sufficient amount of breath to speak. The words disappeared as soon as they left my mouth.

"How come, Lisa?" they demanded, unanimous. "How come?" Shadows broke away from larger shadows to join the crowd, faces I didn't recognize.

I ran, and though I did not look back, I knew they moved along the path of the labyrinth as one body, a beast with multiple heads spitting out the same unanswerable phrase: "How come? How come?" At each sharp turn they were nearly on top of me, pulling at my clothes with fingers that, thank God, I yanked my shirt out of. "How come? How come?" Panic lent me enough energy for a sprint to the exit.

I was several yards out onto the lawn at the back of the house before I knew I'd made it out of the labyrinth. The wall of hedges was behind me, the open portal now displaying only gray oncoming night, the shadows of hedges beyond. I stood wanting to suffocate myself with this new air around me. Certainly the trample of feet would explode from the opening, the questions, *the* question.

None came.

Panting at my car door, I knew I'd gotten out of the

labyrinth but I had not escaped. I turned the key in the ignition. All of them, I knew, would be out here, waiting, demanding the same thing.

And how could I explain myself?

Paper Lanterns

There were no windows in the Gamesroom. I only knew when night had fallen by the time display on the computer. I'd been standing at the counter for over three hours, but the amount of time my mind inhabited the same space as my body probably added up to about ten minutes or so.

Once in a while I glanced over at the nine-ball game Donovan was running with his friends, at the eighth table in the corner. Pool didn't interest me when there weren't any girls around. There were hardly ever any girls around.

I brushed chalk and dandruff off the green felt tables. Over on the big screen TV in the corner of the room, the same video by Savage Garden played and was inevitably followed by that black-and-white hit by the Goo Goo Dolls. I walked through the arcade room, lifted a paper cup from between the Indiana Jones pinball machine and Time Crisis while the screen light strobes of sky blue and pink pulsed around me, sound-tracked by Street Fighter II and Bubble Bobble. The scene reminded me of the red paper lanterns Angie had asked me put up outside the house, the kind that plugged in.

Someone cracked the balls on Donovan's table, the start of a new game. I stepped outside, near the row of bank machines and the stairs that led to the Campus Center auditorium. I lit a cigarette and watched the line of lights that illuminated nothing but the sidewalk from Kuykendall to Dole Street.

There was no Hotel Street bar, no restaurant smoking section at 3:00 am, no Makiki apartment at sundown that was lonelier than the University of Hawai'i campus after hours on a Friday night. A quick look around caught you unawares with its desolation. It was the last day before spring break. My roommates at the Kaimuki house had planned a party that night. Angie had asked for paper lanterns above the patio, and

I'd hammered them into place while standing on a chair.

I smoked and above me, above all of us, the Manoa clouds rolled in for the evening. Whether it rained made little difference to me — I felt like getting drunk, nothing more. As I stared into my own smoke, a figure — a hunchbacked shadow — shuddered in the light all busted up through the limbs and leaves of a windblown tree on the other side of the lawn. What I thought I saw was a person not moving toward me, not away. Somehow it walked in place, stationary. For a second, a sense a dread filled the hollowness of the Friday night, the same kind of horror I'd grappled with during strong spells of THC. The shadow I'd feared all my life had emerged. But it didn't approach. When I threw my cigarette into the loading zone, the shadow had moved on, a trick of the low light.

I lit another cigarette, not so surprised that weird appearances when I was halfway high could still startle me. Beyond my line of vision, past Kennedy Theater and Jefferson Hall, was the Japanese garden, where I'd taken dates some nights. The garden was prettiest when they had the paper lanterns up, little red balls that made everything appear lustful and mine. Under red paper lanterns anything could look beautiful.

I took twenty dollars out of the ATM: a case of beer

after work. When the cigarette was done I went back into the video game room and unplugged each of the machines until it was completely dark. The only sound in the Gamesroom was the cracking of a new set of balls, Donovan and his friends and their repetitive commentary.

"Ho, you hustling me or what?"

"You lucky, hah!"

Someone had left a *Ka Leo O Hawaii* on the counter, and I flipped through to an exposé on secret places on the UH campus where students had gone for sex. That they would let this kind of shit get published was the reason why everyone held the paper in contempt. I had yet to make love to anyone.

A Mace and half a Lenny Kravitz video had passed when the guy in the wheelchair rolled into the Gamesroom. I'm not good with handicapped people. Aside from a blind kid with whom I rode the bus in middle school, I'd never spent any time with them, never really been around them, never saw them from a distance of less than four feet. Crippled to me was worse and more fearsome than death. Whenever I'd complained to my mom about how shitty my life was at this time or that, her response was "Well, you could be some paraplegic in a wheelchair. Count your blessings."

And as far as handicapped folks go, this guy was a mess. He was dressed in a yellow polo shirt and blue shorts that exposed his legs, near thin as broom handles, ringed tube socks pulled up almost to the knee. One of his hands was raised on the arms of his wheelchair, his fingers going up and down involuntarily, as if he was trying to keep track of an alternating series of numbers. The other arm was seemingly at rest, its wrist curved into a raptor claw above the wheelchair's control stick. His head bobbed in place as his mouth opened and closed, his chin pulled into his throat.

I thought he'd come into the wrong place. I was likely in the wrong place myself. I stared at the comics in the *Ka Leo* and made an effort not to look at him. As there was nothing for him to do here, I figured he'd just roll back out the door.

"I need to go—" he said, the words so labored each sounded like its own statement, not part of a sentence.

I looked up and saw that the man's eyes, even though his head was uncontrolled, were clear and fixed on mine.

"To the bathroom," he concluded.

"What?"

"I need to go—to the bathroom," he repeated.

I noticed a two-day's growth of stubble on his cheeks.

"The bathroom's just over there," I said, pointing toward the exit. "You'll see the sign."

When the man spoke, it was like he was trying to chew and swallow something very challenging. Only the vocal cords at the back of his throat seemed compliant with his thoughts. "I can't — myself. Please help."

"Help push?" I stepped from behind the counter.

The man's curled fingers brushed the joystick at the arm of his chair and he moved backwards several inches. "Help — go."

I stopped. I've never claimed to be the quickest of thinkers. "You need help using the bathroom."

"Yes," he said in a patient, drawn out syllable.

I didn't think it rude when I turned away and walked to Donovan's table. If Donovan hadn't been there, I would have closed the place a half-hour earlier, I would be in an aisle at Foodland figuring whether it was Miller Lite or Bud Light that was on sale. If someone in the Gamesroom needed help using the bathroom, it was Donovan's fault and Donovan's responsibility.

I gave a nod to the group and pulled Donovan to the side.

"What's up?" Donovan said, his cue propped between us. "You ready for us to finish up here?"

"Look, you see that guy over there?"

"He's the only guy in the place. Of course I see him."

"He needs to go to the bathroom."

Donovan shrugged. "So?"

"He needs to go to the bathroom."

Donovan looked at him again. "Oh," he said, and set his cue against the wall. "Let's do it then." He began to walk to the wheelchair. Relief dropped through me, leaving only the slightest residue of disgust.

Donovan turned back to me. "With the two of us, we can take care of this quick. Come on, man."

Someone racked up another set of balls.

We walked slowly on each side of the man in the wheelchair as he motored toward the men's room. Approaching the door, Donovan skipped ahead, holding it open as the man rolled onto the white tile. I caught my reflection in the mirror as I followed them. It looked like all the muscles had disappeared from my face, all the bone structure gone soft. I was about to do something I didn't want to do.

Donovan pulled the door to the handicapped stall, and the man reversed until he was just before the toilet, Donovan and I on either side of him.

"Go back until you're right next to it," Donovan told him.

A few more jerking grabs at the joystick and he was where Donovan thought he should be.

"We'll get his pants down once we move him off his

seat. I'll grab his legs here — "

At last I stepped forward, and took the man by his thin legs and quivering back.

"Thank you," was all he said, looking at neither of us.

When we had him on the toilet seat, I followed Donovan again and dug my fingers into the elastic bands of his shorts and underwear, and we pulled both lopsided down his legs. His white briefs were not new.

"Ah," Donovan said, as if something had just occurred to him.

Between the man's useless legs his dick, larger than any I'd ever seen, stood rigid from his groin. As if, almost, making a fist at us. The skin of it, darker than the skin of his thighs, bulged with veins along its length.

We'd gotten him into position. I didn't know where the man's eyes were anymore. Donovan looked at me and swallowed.

#

I carried a twelve pack of Bud Light cans on the handlebars of my bike on the hill up Pahoa. I kept thinking about something Nick's girlfriend had told me earlier that day. She was from Peru, and there were all these stray cats in the neighborhood where she'd lived with her mom. One day her mom just up and poisoned all of the cats, buried them in an empty lot a couple blocks away. Nick and I thought it was too bad for the cats. She said it was probably better for them. Nick's girlfriend was none too fond of cats. Nor other people, really. Maybe that's why they broke up a few months later.

Between Sixth and Seventh Avenue, I lost a pedal and the beer went down before the bike. Two cans exploded on the curb and sprayed out to the road. The rest were mostly dented, so I dropped them back into the broken box and pushed the bike up the hill with the beer in the other arm. A trail of blood started slowly from my elbow.

Our house then, built on a hill, had two levels, the second floor built on the top and the kitchen, alcove, and three bedrooms constructed on the lower part of the hill. Upstairs, I saw bodies moving along lit windows, the girls getting ready for the party. I walked past, down into the kitchen. Outside the kitchen was our concrete patio, above which the lit paper lanterns blew in a wet breeze.

I ran the faucet over my elbow at the kitchen sink. I'd fallen so many times, these things hardly felt anymore. I flipped on the radio on the counter boom box, the only component that worked since the CD player and the tape player had gone dead. I recognized the tune as "Every Time We Say Goodbye," which was completely fucking unsuitable for any party I would have gone to then. But I didn't change the station.

I took the beer to my bedroom and lay on my bed, sucking down a can while holding my arm high, so as to not stain the sheets. I wasn't sure I was all that interested in a party anymore. I heard footsteps just outside my room, and Angie's voice in the hall. "Get your asses out here, people. The guests have arrived."

I was probably drinking beers on my bed for an hour before I left my room. People—some I knew, most I didn't—lined the halls with beers or red solo cups. A friend of a friend of someone had decided to be bartender at the kitchen table, and poured drinks to order. I just wandered around with warm beers and a scab on my elbow. "Every Time We Say Goodbye" was now someone playing Bruce Springsteen on my record player in the alcove. I saw someone else wearing my shirt—he must have pulled it from the wardrobe outside my room—and instead of getting pissed off I said he could have it. I didn't feel like anything was really mine. He spent the rest of the night putting on my clothes.

We didn't smoke cigarettes in the house, but we did smoke pot. During a never-ending joint someone remarked on how fucking crazy "Thunder Road" was, and I said that it was a moment that could never be replicated.

I went outside for a cigarette. Everyone was huddled

under the roof of the patio, to keep away from the rain streaming down on all sides. The paper lanterns had dissolved, torn to shit by the wind, and when I looked up I found nothing beautiful about them anymore. They were nothing but light.

Waikiki Wedding

It was an invitation to a wedding. Thick paper stock, one sheet, colored in blue and the orangish tinge of sunset. I figured that a cousin or out-of-touch friend had surrendered him or herself to whom they thought they could bear for the rest of their lives. Presumably because there was nothing better to do. Marriage was a fate I wished no one, especially since it diminished the stock of eligible aging women I might have otherwise enticed into my isolated orbit.

"Brian Kam," it read, "invites you to share in the pleasure of his union. July 24 at the Hyatt Regency,

Honolulu." An email address and a phone number, both of which I'd known as far back as I can remember, had been printed for RSVP purposes.

I'd been Brian's best friend since our freshman year at Castle High School. I'd last had several pitchers of beer with him at at a bar on Kapahlulu four days ago. As I recall, a rough and unproductive night of few women. The conversation had been built from a reconfiguration of things we always talked about—TV shows, old professional wrestlers, and the Beatles. I was damn certain that he'd never mentioned meeting anyone, much less asking for some unlucky woman's hand in marriage.

Who would he, *could* he, marry, anyway? The girl with the tattoo that covered her back? The one about whom he complained of B.O.? Brian left all the women he dated. He faded himself out of this fix and that, little disappearances that always led to uncomfortable reunions at our favorite bars. Brian was a disgrace when it came to matters of the heart. That he might actually find someone before I did galled me.

A joke, I thought. An expensive, unfunny joke. Having wedding invitations made and mailed just to fuck with his friends wasn't beyond Brian, though. I called him right away.

Voicemail. I tried another number.

"So you got the invitation," Reynold said.

"Yeah. What kind of bullshit is he trying to pull?"

"No bullshit. I talked to him yesterday."

"What, he met somebody in a day and now he's got his wedding planned? Who the hell is he marrying?"

"You didn't read the invitation?"

"Yeah, I read it. I didn't see a name I recognized."

"You didn't see a name, period. There was no other name."

"No name? So who's Brian marrying next month?"

"He's not marrying anyone, man. No, I'm saying that wrong. He's marrying himself."

"Horseshit."

"No, Cyril, not horseshit. This is gonna happen."

"I—can that happen? I mean, is it even legal?"

"It better not be fucking legal," Reynold said. "If it's not legal for me to get married to who I want to get married to, it better be a fucking crime for Brian Kam to marry himself."

"This is not a joke?"

"Brian just wants to have a honeymoon. You know he does weird shit sometimes."

"I don't get it," I said.

"Look, it's just gonna be a paid-for party with booze. I've already RSVP'd."

At the university the next day, I did my usual thing at

Kuykendall Hall—a large cup of coffee sipped through the hours, long past the point of palatability; one class of undergraduates whose impassivity to "The Beast in the Jungle" seemed to me hostile; department-related emails; frequent visits to bathroom, and just as many to the Web, wondering who had commented on my blog post about *A Voyage to Arcturus* (no one, as a matter of fact); another curry lunch in the office, doors closed and windows open, where I watched through the jalousies the tanned, toned youth in the courtyard; and the last class of the day, when the last cold mouthful of coffee inspired me to ask the class nothing, and instead I finally told them what my interpretation of "The Beast in the Jungle" was, and by their grim responses it chilled whatever warmth they expected to leave the room with. Enough coffee and a man can believe he never had a soul.

The whole hall was clearing out, a slow sad coda to another day's end. As on most Thursdays, I didn't have the heart to return to the empty floor on which my office was located, so I took the stairs toward Manoa Gardens to meet Brian before his class.

Brian, through web ingenuity and preternatural understanding of how digital information is processed most efficiently by end users, had acquired riches and means far beyond the reach of his peers. For some reason, he'd chosen to continue his friendships, hence me. After his success with an application he'd sold to Apple, he retired to pursue the higher education he'd dismissed as an undergraduate in theatre.

In other words, he was loaded, and had nothing better to do than pile up degrees at the University of Hawai'i. His friends and family admired his loyalty to us and to the places where he liked to swim, places he had blown past on his skateboard, places in which he had smoked from a one-hitter, hit on girls, drank. At the same time, we thought it was completely fucking bonkers he hadn't grown up and out of here. He hadn't invested. He hadn't changed his style. He was still drinking five-dollar Bud Light pitchers with me on Fridays, thirty-two ouncers at Manoa Gardens on Thursdays, buying seasons worth of DVDs, living in a pretty cage near Ala Moana. And if it seems strange to you that this man of wealth had not found someone, man or woman, with whom to share his comfort and cleverness and lack of gumption—I have yet to address Joy, the young woman whom Brian loved, and who died.

Manoa Gardens was an ugly cement courtyard with mismatched metal tables, all in various stages of rust, set in the ground. Occasionally doves would land near your feet and pick at grains of rice. The only good thing about the joint was that it was close, and you could drink.

Brian had already swallowed a quarter of his plastic cup's red ale when I saw him. He nodded at me, and I went into the bar to get a drink.

"You're breaking your mother's heart, carrying on like this," I said, setting an IPA on the table. "Desecrating the sacred institution of marriage."

"My mom's doing hula at the reception," Brian said.

"This is really happening?"

"Really happening."

"Why? What kind of person marries himself? I mean, you end up just spending all this money for a joke."

"It'll be a good party, at least."

"But why even frame a good party as a wedding? You don't think you can find someone to marry? I mean, you're a normal, average looking guy."

"Thanks."

"With no obvious deformities. It's not like you're a leper or—I mean, is it a penis thing? Some kind of penis thing?"

Brian laughed. "You're taking this too seriously, man. This isn't some kind of commitment to be alone the rest of my life. This is supposed to be fun. I know it's kind of weird, but it'll be fun. Come on, man. Everyone's on board."

I took a large drink, gasped, and set the cup down. "So

this whole thing isn't about Joy, then?"

"Nah, man. It's got nothing to do with her."

Total crock of bullshit, I thought.

Brian had known Joy for three years, seven months, and six and three-eighths of a day, according to his estimate. Seven years ago, he'd seen her at an open mic reciting a poem about prison fisting as an expression of love. Brian (in his troubadour phase then) followed a little later, singing a ballad acapella about an open hand reaching out from the sun to lift a boat into the cosmos. I'd been in the audience with a fixed expression of distaste. It wasn't just that both of them referred to hands as a means of transcendence that I saw it coming.

I am violently jealous when a friend connects with a pretty woman. It's immature, it's futile and it's sad, but when it comes to the shameful delusions to which all of us are susceptible, my own megalomaniacal, misogynistic, possessive delusion is that all girls are meant for me. In the old days I fell in love every minute. But something later told me that I would have to stop myself, that it was beginning to be unseemly, pathetic.

In this case, watching Joy watch Brian from the audience through the amber glaze of an Anchor Steam and the low lights inflated me with a selfless sense that I wanted to have these two love each other. Just by their unmet eyes from across the room I knew that these two beings' lives would be far sadder had they not the opportunity to commiserate, cohabitate, copulate.

"Splendid!" I cried before Brian had finished his final chorus. I'd heard the song ad nauseum at Brian's apartment, and it was no great disappointment to the audience that Brian's performance was abbreviated. The half-hearted applause, barely audible over the chatter, brought Brian's ballad to a close, and he looked confused as I caught him around the shoulders with a beer for his hand and led him to the table of Joy, who sat with her taciturn friend.

"This world can bear only so many geniuses," I said to my small crowd. I was, for once, under no self-inflicted pressure, and attacked my role with glee. "Their truth telling is a rough medicine. Ladies, I give you Brian Kam."

It was a stupid thing to say, but I'd spared Brian from having to come up with something himself. Brian and Joy began talking at once and so naturally I thought I hadn't really introduced them at all, but that they'd known each other from time before. It was a rushed kind of talk, beyond the comprehension of an observing third party. So I succumbed to a solid ass kicking in pool by the friend.

And it came to pass that Brian had found his Other. This was Socrates, by way of Plato, by way of Hedwig kind of stuff, in which disparate limbs are fused to others to generate a purer, more beautiful being. I no longer knew Brian in the same way I'd known him—he had, with his love, become Brian and Joy, a manifestation of refracted identities. They laughed a lot. They hugged a lot.

One year, three months, and eight days after they met, Joy went to the doctor to address a recurring migraine. This turned out to be a neoplasm roughly the size and shape of a fully masticated pack of Big League Chew, just under the shell of her skull. No one said die, then—our era of medicine had advanced so that a brain tumor was par for the course in some ways, as easily fixable as scurvy or the scarlet fever. I've already mentioned that it did, in fact, get her.

I could go on and on about how they were able to be well together, to say they were happy and were actually happy in that smug, oblivious, pure state without guilt or apprehension or second guessing. To avoid further mawkishness I have one anecdote that comes to mind.

I'd gone over to Brian's house late one night after the bars, thinking I might be able to procure an eighth of pot. I knocked on his door—this was when Brian still lived in a shitty motel-style apartment on Kapahulu—and when no one answered, I used the copy of the key he made for me to help myself to his stash in the counter above the kitchen sink.

With only the sodium streetlights to guide me through his kitchen, I found the baggie and pinched off a nice chunk. As I felt through his drawers for a ziploc, I heard voices through the partially closed bedroom door. I turned, noticed the light was on. Very quickly, I tried to come up with something I could brandish as a weapon. When you're drunk, gags like this make more sense.

I crept to the doorway with a cucumber in my fist. Looking through the door's crack, I saw Brian and Joy in bed—not intimate yet, or not anymore. Joy had her hands on her belly and laughed a few seconds or so, which caused Brian to crack up, interrupting whatever he'd been saying to her. Seconds later, I saw he was reading to her. It was hard to focus on the title of the book, bleary as I was, but the cover was a god-awful picture of a Victorian woman or something, and as I listened to Brian speaking in a French accent, I realized he was reading *Madame Bovary*. Together, they'd turned *Madame Bovary* into a comedy.

"But why marry yourself?" I said to Brian. "You've got money. You may not be a Rock Hudson or Montgomery Clift, but you're certainly no Charles Laughton."

"I'm not saying I have to stay married to myself forever, man. It's just a fun thing to do."

I looked at him. He was actually going through with it.

This wasn't the Brian who had never grown beyond his friends, or his time at college, or the bars on Thursdays. This wasn't the Brian who had been floating for god knows how long. This was a Brian who wanted to do something, who *wanted* something. "Well, okay," I said. "So, am I the best man, or what?"

"That's a negative," Brian said. "Kelley's my best man."

"Your sister?" I shook my head. "Jesus, you really don't give a shit about anything."

The weeks leading up to Brian's wedding, I was overwhelmed with work for the summer semester. I didn't see anyone much. I couldn't believe I'd taken on another class. They were always more work than you thought they would be, and the students were eager to matriculate through their English courses twice as fast as if they'd taken the class during the fall. Naturally, they were twice as uninterested in the material. I did make a trip out to Sears at Ala Moana for the fitting of a cream-colored tuxedo rental which, though adjustable, was going to look baggy and unfetching on me. I briefly considered going out to search for a date to the wedding, but the circumstances were too strange to try and explain it to anyone I just met.

A week before the wedding, Kelley sent out an email to everyone announcing that she was throwing Brian's bachelor party at Smith's Union Bar on Hotel Street. Back then, Smith's Union was far worse than the place it is now. If you imagine that some bars are young and healthy and vibrant, and others are decrepit but still firm of mind and body, and that others are sick with a disease that can never be cured, Smith's Union was the equivalent of a bar in permanent hospice, a usually catatonic, barely breathing establishment that, if given the right crowd, could sometimes have flashes of clarity. The Hotel Street irregulars who otherwise had no place to go drank Bud Lights on ice there. Elderly folks, lifers in booze who had lost their ability to speak went there. I'd seen a man with a bandage that covered what once was his nose there. Bald women, and no small population of people without teeth. What Smith's Union had going for it was two dollar beers—which the bar often comped if you stuck around long enough—one of last remaining non-MP3, oldies-based jukeboxes, and karaoke songs a dollar apiece.

Reynold, his boyfriend Daniel, and I were the first ones at the bar, with Kelley driving Brian down after a big sister-financed dinner at Macaroni Grill. I ordered a round of bourbon shots (the beer backs were provided gratis) and loosened up the old pipes with a version of "You Don't Know Me." My standards are Ray Charles and Jim Croce ballads.

Daniel followed with a soulful, applause-capturing

rendition of Cecelio and Kapono's "About You," and Reynold showed his chops in a spirited performance of "Africa." More drinks appeared before us on the bar, and then Rick and K and Lon came through the doors, and finally Kelley with Brian en tote. Each song that appeared on the TV screen and the speakers seemed to contain the sum total of the world's blues and ecstasy, and soon I was off the bar stool and dancing between the tables, drawing old women up from their chairs, hugging strangers. Brian, his fingers clutching a new full glass of something each time I looked at him, shouted "I'm getting married!" every fifteen minutes, to which everyone in the bar toasted and guzzled.

During one old man's pitch perfect rendering of "Fifty Ways to Leave Your Lover," Brian put his arm around my shoulders, breathing wetly in my face. "What am I doing man?" he said. "I don't know if I can go through with this." Indecision, fear, inability to follow through—that was the Brian I knew.

"You can't get cold feet now," I yelled. "This means too much to too many people."

"I just wanted something—I don't know man. I just wanted something I thought could make me whole."

"You wanted to be a hole?" Reynold said, laying his hands on each of our shoulders. "Just cool it in the bathroom, there's sure to be some action sooner or later." The bathroom was a closet-sized space in which a zinc basin with faucet served as a urinal. Washing one's hands was catch as catch can.

"I'm getting married!" Brian cried, and several dozen glasses, the equivalent of fifty or so dollars, were dumped down gullets that were already numb and could hardly stand for more.

The wedding ceremony took place on the brief grass plain between Kapiolani Park and Waikiki Beach, with the wedding party—Kelley, Reynold, Ryan, K and I—standing shoulder to shoulder in a diagonal line in the sun. Brian couldn't have picked a better day for a wedding. Despite its brightness against my cream-colored coat, it was like the sunlight and the wind had fused into some gentler, cooler element that made standing in place a pleasure.

Nearby, Brian's family and their friends stood in a crowd looking toward the empty spot where Brian was to give his vows to himself. It was a small group of invitees, but I was surprised at how many people did show—these days, I suppose, more people are willing to be cool with what others are wont to do.

The priest—or whoever Brian had hired for the gig—still hadn't showed when Brian, dressed in a white suit that recalled John Lennon in 1969, walked the patch of grass designated as the aisle. Rather than imbuing the walk with a practiced kind of significance, he moved through the blob of folks he'd invited giving handshakes and kisses before he took his place facing Kelley.

A guy in an Aloha shirt no one recognized wandered over from the direction of the beach and turned to Kelley. "Kam wedding?"

"This is the place," Kelley said. "Our groom stands before you."

"Great," the man said. He held out his too-tanned hand to Brian. "Name's Earl. Were you thinking a Buddhist kind of thing, Christian? I can also do your general specific, non-spiritual 'we are linked by the bond of eternal love' kind of thing."

"But that's under the assumption that human beings house immortal souls, which would imply spirituality," I said, stepping forward a little out of my place in the diagonal.

"Well, maybe," Earl said. "But when I've tried to address decay, disease and death in a set of vows, everyone tends to get bummed out."

"Just shoot from the hip," Brian said.

"Shoot from the hip, while speaking from the heart," Earl replied. "Got it. Now we're just waiting for the bride?"

"No bride," Kelley said.

"Ah, the other groom, then."

"No groom," Brian said.

"So—who is it exactly that's getting married?"

"Me," Brian said.

"Him to him," I piped in, pointing at Brian twice to avoid confusion.

"This is, well, this is a new kind of thing—"

"You can make it quick."

"Right." Earl took a step back, placed his hands together, and gathered his big voice unto him. He had not removed the pair of sunglasses he showed up in. "Ladies and gentlemen, we face in our lives everyday situations that perplex and often pain us. One person behaves in a way we don't understand, and we react in fear, sometimes disgust, and yes, sometimes pure loathing. But is it our burden to judge that which displeases us? I say to you, one man's abomination is another man's grace."

Kelley had begun laughing in her hand.

"With that I stand here as a witness to the love that—"

"Brian," Brian said.

"Brian wishes to express to himself in front of the seas, the skies, the trees—"

"The garbage cans, the bacteria, the pollution," Kelley

muttered.

"The sands, the grasses and the people who love him, for whatever reason — and those reasons are, may I add, non-transferable, as one person's love for someone else may be, if I may, absolutely freaking inconceivable to someone else, like someone who doesn't know him."

"Wrap it up," Brian said. "The fee was a lump sum."

"And by that, what is there left to say? By the power vested in me — actually, I have no real power to bear witness to a man marrying himself — but, for the sake of concluding whatever you see before you, I announce to you the marriage of Brian to Brian. Not another Brian, but the same Brian. You may do as you wish."

While we all applauded and Brian waved, Kelley took Earl, who had already turned back to the beach whence he came, and explained everything.

The reception — which the now-at-ease Earl attended, once he'd gotten word of the open bar — took place at the Hyatt, just a few blocks down the street. Our party walked en masse to the hotel, each of us offering in ironic fashion what we thought were the best of our wishes. I hung back with Reynold and Daniel, the three of us taking turns at a glass pipe Reynold drew from the rented pocket of his tuxedo.

At the ballroom, before anyone took their assigned

seats, a great queue formed in front of the liquor people, and their fish bowl of tip cash soon overflowed with dollars and fives. Per the reception schedule, drinks would last from 4:00 pm to 8:00 pm, which would more than allow for a good slog through a variety of beverages. It was if Brian had planned it out that everyone would forget what we were there for, while we were there. The buffet line, which at first guests approached with trays and plates and lifted tongs and plastic serving spoons became, after two hours of frequent toasts to nothing, a messy trough around which the shirt sleeved and barefoot guests grazed, plucking and shoving into mouths.

Brian's mother, according to tradition, took the center of the ballroom for her hula sometime after eight. What transpired after a few seconds of attempting the dance was the most offensive, obscene, and possibly hurtful performance I'd ever witnessed. Brian's mother, forgone by that point, had transmogrified into some kind of knotty demon in a muumuu, expressing in movements and speech a debased, perverted sexuality, gross racism, and death threats to certain parties who had attended the ceremony. And yes, her boobs were exposed, though only one at a time, burlesque-style.

No dance with Brian's dad followed, nor dance between mother and son, because mom had reached a level of transcendence and was no longer saying, or thinking anything really, other than "well, all right," a blessing she administered with a slow wave of her hand, slumped in her chair. Kelley followed, giving a best man speech that not once mentioned Brian, and was more of an anecdote illustrating how shitty her own wedding had been, how much less fun, much to the chagrin of her husband in the audience (the two kids were at home with the other grandma, who wanted nothing to do with the travesty). It started off funny, descended to humorous, further down to amusing, then somewhat shocking, then enervating, and set all of its observers, most of whom now lacked the will to yell out "shut the fuck up!" just to see what would happen, into a state of irredeemable grimness. In other words, the event, the culmination of what was probably a bad idea in the first place, had at last hit its full potential of awfulness, and the alcohol, which had first electrified the guests, had pulled away the veil of the bride to reveal a great hole, nothing.

With that Brian took to the center of the ballroom and at once, as confused and distressed as they had become over the course of the night, the guests seemed to remember this event was supposed to be a celebration. The music, which had been going most of the evening on the periphery of my awareness, stopped, and the horrible inertness of silence swallowed all of our voices in a smothering lurch forward.

Brian, in the lights, looked tired, but he didn't look dead yet. Seconds later we heard low electric guitar strings plucked over the speakers, followed by a baritone saxophone. Brian began to slow dance, sans partner, first in a stiff but rapidly fluid manner, to "Don't Look Back."

I looked around the room. The smiles had begun, and not the happy for you smiles but the nasty smiles that cut up the face when some asshole makes a fool of himself. Each second and Brian's face became more severe and yet detached, as if each step taught him that he would be, forever, the sole inhabitant of his body. He had married himself — he had come to grips with being himself, and being by himself. The smiles dropped off of faces, and we all looked on, now only interested and sad. Joy was no longer present. This was now only Brian. This was someone who had loved as though it was his only function, and then that love was useless. This was a man who had made it to the other side of grief. And then we all ceased being interested, and were only sad. The greatest shame is in witnessing the misfortune of others.

The song ended. We all knew we needed to go. Brian to his rented hotel room, the rest of us to cabs and scheduled rides. There was nothing to say to one another. We saw something we would never see again, something none of us wanted to see again. Attendant to grace is embarrassment.

Walking by the buffet, I broke open a dinner roll and shoved a chunk of beef inside, eating it dripping as I staggered out the lobby of the hotel toward the waves that soothed and mocked and judged all the actions of men. The importance of their message was lost on me.

The Ala Wai at Night

When Lev moved into the Summer Palace, his mother was dead. He knew certain parts of himself would no longer be helpful in getting through the rest of his life. Nighttimes he'd go out to the lanai and stare at the Ala Wai flowing below. Once in a while, a lone kayak would break up the canal's still reflection of lit hotels and apartment buildings.

The Summer Palace was an apartment complex off Atkinson, behind the Convention Center. Lev rented a corner one-bedroom on the seventh floor, living alone for the first time in his thirty-two years. Previously, he'd lived with his mother in a house in Kaimuki next to the freeway. He was the only one of his siblings who would. The good son, though not totally without resentment, while Pam and Clyde founded their own homes with people they were in love with.

By now, Lev was too old to enjoy blasting Cream or Led Zeppelin in his apartment. Too scared to spend hours in his living room sucking on a hash pipe. What should have been new and liberating instead came at him foreign and overwhelming. His mother's things were no longer his things. He hung prints on the walls, paid a furniture store to move a leather sofa to a spot in front of the television, and filled a matching armoire and bookshelf with clothes and books. He found that when he was home too long he heard a piano playing from somewhere.

The phantom piano player was probably a seventh-grader endlessly practicing "Clair de Lune" upstairs, but it wouldn't have been the first time Lev heard music in his head. He looked for excuses to leave his apartment. When he wasn't at work he went out walking, or sat in coffee shops, or browsed the last of the used bookstores in Honolulu. He'd put together a wooden table from Home Depot, but took his meals at the kitchen counter, standing up.

At work, Lev worried whether he turned the coffeepot off, or if he turned the stove off after breakfast, or if he should have unplugged the toaster, or if he turned off the lamp above his bed that, given enough time, would probably set his mattress on fire. When she was alive, Lev would call his mother and ask her to check all the appliances. More than once she told him she turned everything off when she'd actually turned them on. She was blind and she tended to forget.

So Lev ate cold cereal and drank instant coffee and only used florescent lights. Still, there were any number of things that could send the whole works into oblivion. When he worried now, there was nothing to do but sit in it all day. He knew the cure was to stop fucking caring, but there's a difference between what someone knows and what someone does. Flashes of panic often struck him while explaining what a supplementary retirement plan could do for a future financial portfolio, or while reconciling a closed federal account. These little flare ups left his mouth dry and his heart running to catch up with something that was long gone.

The radio at work played nothing but news programs, which was soothing because it made him feel like the only person on planet Earth. Lev heard the tinny reports of world affairs while typing on the keyboard or reading emails that were only situationally important—meaning, they had no relevance whatsoever except in a very narrow context that 99.999999% of the world neither knew nor cared about. "Could you please forward the biosafety requirements to Theresa?" "What was my sick leave balance as of December

2010?" "Was that PO ever generated for the subcontract with UCSD?"

Most of the news stories over the radio were thrillingly bleak, hopeless, tale after tale of acute and articulate misery. Lev imagined the news broadcasts were from a troubled planet far away, where nations were forever on the brink of war or economic collapse, especially vulnerable to frequent hurricanes, floods, and earthquakes. It had so little in common with what he witnessed everyday he was convinced it was all fictional.

"How can you keep listening to that stuff?" Charlene said as she dropped a folder onto his desk. Signatures from the CFO approving payroll. The last thing he was about to do was try and explain it to Charlene.

"Well, it's," Lev began. It was the radio thing that made him feel okay moment to moment. Lev smiled at Charlene, comforted that she wasn't all that invested in his response anyway.

In the mail room Lev found himself staring at the wall of mail slots, cubby holes of varying size that were either empty or full. For the third time that day, Lev's slot was empty.

"Well, hello sir," Kate said, though not as respectfully as it may have seemed, because Kate had never seriously called anyone sir in her life. "Haven't seen you around these parts in a while. Backpacking through Europe, have we?"

Kate was one of a double Kate in the office. There were two of almost everybody: two Kates, two Charlenes, two Eds, two Michaels, two Nancys, a Michele and a Michelle. This Kate took great pains in besmirching the reputation of her namesake. She was usually stricken with a temporary illness on Mondays or Fridays, and her output, Lev had heard, was always sloppy. Lev liked her because he didn't have to work with her. Kate was especially good at popping into offices and talking about weekends.

"Jesus, Lev," Kate said as he turned to her. "Just get back from Dachau or something?"

"I wasn't on vacation," Lev told her. "My mother she"—don't say passed away, Lev told himself, do not say passed away—"she passed away."

"For Christ's sake, Lev," Kate said, and she looked at him, for a moment more distraught than he felt, before she threw an arm around him and pulled him close. "I mean, how can you possibly worry about any of this shit?" She threw the stack of mail she had not yet distributed in the corner of the counter. "How about I buy you a cup of coffee, okay? This is like the *last* thing you should be thinking about now." As Lev followed her out of the room, he wondered who would have to the sort the mail she'd left behind.

"You know, Lev," Kate said as she sipped at her coffee, "I know exactly what you're going through, believe it or not." They'd walked downstairs to the cafe, empty except for one straggler from the outside world who had found a place to sit. Lev used his cup to warm his hands. "My mom," Kate said, "died two years ago. A year and eight months actually."

"I'm sorry to hear that," Lev said, asking himself if there was a statute of limitations on these kinds of programmed responses.

Kate shrugged. "No need to be sorry. She had a great life. Danced, loved to travel — went to twenty, twenty-five different countries. Countries, Lev! I haven't even been to that many states." She shook her head, took another drink of her coffee. "She was a funny lady. What was your mom like?"

"She liked jazz," Lev said. After a few moments, he added, "Well, she was blind."

Kate nodded. "And were you — the primary caregiver?"

He'd never thought about himself in that way. What the hell did primary caregiver mean? It was more like they hung out a lot.

When she was alive, his mother would sit on the same side of the couch every evening as he walked in, the radio's news segment just finished and the classical concert series scheduled to begin. In most cases she didn't speak until the end of the symphony. Lev used the time to change his clothes and make dinner. He wanted to make the dishes she made for her children when she could cook, but ended up frying something in a pan. His mother was congenial to canned food, like every other old person: Vienna sausage, spam, tuna, sardines.

Lev would situate his mother's plate, utensils and glass of water so she knew where they were. After the symphony, classical music would play until the jazz program. At times, Lev's mother was so attuned to the music she held her fork aloft for several minutes, mouth open, waiting for a sequence to conclude. What she truly felt during any particular moment of the day she found impossible to convey. Eventually she had made up her mind not to try.

When she did find her words, Lev's mother asked him when he'd be married, when he'd have children like Pam and Clyde. Some nights Lev would take her to walk around the block if she wasn't too tired, or they'd go to the market so she could feel the fruit. But the engines of mopeds and the stopping and starting of buses made her nervous. They didn't stay out long.

Every other Wednesday Lev took an hour off of work and drove his mother to Kapiolani Medical Center for an examination, some kind of blood draw, always the same test. In the elevator to the doctor's office on the ninth floor they'd stand in the corner and Lev would hold her by the elbow. When the medical assistant took her at the office, Lev would brush his mother's hair out of her pale eyes and kiss her on the cheek. A regular dose of this and anyone would be prepared for death.

"Gosh, Lev, you gotta get out," Kate said, nodding as if she agreed with herself. Then she began to shake her head. "Seriously. It was the best thing I could have done. Be around people. Laugh. Do stupid things. You have brothers, or sisters—I mean, how are they taking it?"

"They kind of have their hands full with their kids," Lev said.

Kate looked him in the eye. "Look, I've got plans with friends this Friday. No, you don't have to make it this big uncomfortable thing—it's not a date, it just a lot of drinking. You drink, don't you? I don't trust a man who doesn't drink."

"Sure," Lev said.

"That's from *Casablanca*. Anyway, you come out with us, Lev. Home Bar, right after work. And I want to buy you at least five shots."

"I don't know if that's a good idea," Lev said.

"Just tell me you'll go," Kate said.

Home Bar wasn't but four blocks from his apartment. "I'll try to make it."

A few minutes later Lev saw Kate going down the stairs with one of the Charlenes, an early lunch.

#

"You forget something?" Pam asked him at the door later that afternoon. Her hair had mostly broken free from her pony tail, strands waving around her face. Pam's oldest son, Wendell, pulled at her leg away from the door while the other son, Greg, cried loudly in the room that used to be Lev's.

Pam and her family had moved into his mother's house shortly after the cremation. She stood at the entrance warily, as if afraid Lev might want to move back in.

"I just wanted to bring this back," Lev said, holding out a framed picture of Monk and John Coltrane with their arms around each other. Lev had given the picture to his mother as a gift before she lost her sight. She liked all of them—Miles, Dexter Gordon, Coleman Hawkins, Art Tatum, Duke—but Monk was her favorite. "I don't know why I took it with me. There's no real place for it." He walked past Pam into the house.

Full boxes lined the hallways and stood in the center of rooms, boxes of his mother's things for storage, and Pam's household goods that would replace all the old things. As he walked through, he found there was no place for Monk and Coltrane here, either.

"Why didn't you just give it away to Goodwill?" Pam said, following him. "What, is it worth something?"

On Friday Lev did go to Home Bar, and Kate bought him at least five shots as she'd promised. At least, because he wasn't exactly sure what followed the rest of the evening. When he woke up in his bed late the next morning, fully clothed, he checked to make sure his credit cards were all still in his wallet. Then he stripped down to his underwear.

He thought he might have kissed someone. But it wasn't Kate, since she'd come with her boyfriend. He thought he might have danced. He thought he might have held his head to a jukebox, trying to force it all the way in. Of course, it wasn't all that which made his head hurt now, but if he kept it straight and didn't focus on any one thing, he could pretend it didn't hurt at all.

Lev walked out to the lanai with the empty glass of water he'd drained on the way there. Against the blinding glare of the sun over the Ala Wai he closed his eyes. It looked a lot different during the day. Lev thought about how, after he'd dropped his mother off at the doctor's, he'd drink coffee on the second floor of the hospital, wondering if this was the Wednesday he'd buy a glazed doughnut. He'd look over at all the tables at the pregnant diabetics, the children in casts, the swaddled newborns, and every one with a complaint or concern, all of them suffering simultaneously. But they all suffered well.

Lev opened his eyes and squinted at the buildings across the canal. Someone was smoking pot, and for the first time in a long while it smelled good. Lev wanted some, but he knew it would make him sick. The phantom piano player started up on "Clair de Lune" again, a constant intro with no end.

But it wasn't Debussy. Bass and low organ rumbled after the opening keys of "Bitches Brew," followed by the shatter of drum and cymbal, musical—if you could call them that—instruments battling towards some kind of order before the return of the rumble, the slow creep of the motif. Lev sat back and thought of Monk, who'd fought Nazis in World War II. He imagined an ashy, mud-spattered tank rolling blindly through a minefield, struggling forward in small increments before the next mine exploded under its treads, then an inevitable barrage of bullets before, unbelievably, the tank righted itself and began to plow forward once again. Miles's trumpet in response brought to mind a ghost bugler inciting a hopeless, solitary charge.

R.O.E.

"Aren't any R.O.E.'s in Fallujah," Markus said. Underneath his seated ass the chair looked tiny, like something he'd pulled from a nursery school. His knees pointed two o'clock and his long hands, for once relaxed, hung between his thighs. When an engine started we all looked through our cigarette smoke to the front of the garage — only Benny, moving a car out to the lot.

"What's R.O.E.'s?" I said, willing, like always, to look like the dumb one.

"Rules of engagement," Markus said. "Rules for

soldiers when they're in battle."

"Got rules for that?" Tony said.

Markus didn't look at him. "Shoot anything that moves. Man, shoot. Woman, shoot."

"Jesus," Normie said. Benny shuffled into the crowd of us from the lot, smiling as if he'd just remembered a dirty joke, his bust-up leg dragging behind. But his face went flat when he saw our faces all smoke and seriousness, listening.

"We were holding the checkpoint on the edge of town," Markus said, slowly extending each of his legs all the way the work bench. "Then I see this car coming through the desert to us. Regular sedan. Two men in the front, man and two kids in the back. Both boys. We stopped them there." Markus pulled his ear and scrubbed his fingers on his chin. "Now, you don't ever see kids without women in Iraq," he said. "Kids are always with women. So we ask them for authorization and they don't have shit. Just start yelling—in that language, you know? Then the asshole in the front reaches for the glove compartment. Shit, we blew that car to pieces. You know what we found in the trunk?"

Christ, I hope it wasn't nothing, I thought.

"Full of fucking land mines," Markus said. "It was a damned miracle a stray bullet didn't hit the back." He got to his feet. Upright he dwarfed all of us. Six-eight. Benny and I had to drive most of the cars in for him because his legs were too long for the Toyotas and Hondas of the world.

"Jesus," Normie said, snubbing out the butt of his Camel Light at the greasy bottom of a tuna can.

"I guess it's my turn again," Markus said, referring to the car that had just pulled up to the garage doors.

"Can you believe that shit?" Tony said, taking his hat off, running his hand through his overgrown hair, then pushing and pulling the brim back over his head so it fit in that particular way. "Dead kids."

"No rules of engagement," Normie said sagely, as if that simple phrase could explain everything.

Markus came back and fell into his kiddie-chair. "Jesus," he said, through his teeth. "Niggah wanted to give me a dollar to check his lights."

We all looked toward the garage doors, wondering who he was talking about, surprised to see a miniature Filipino man slide back onto his Cutlass Supreme. Not many people talked like that in Hawai'i, used the word "niggah."

He'd come from Atlanta by way of Iraq, serving a tour in Afghanistan and two more in Fallujah, before it was annihilated. He had temporary housing on the Marine base and, with no wife and nothing better to do, took a job in Ogata's Auto as the lowest level mechanic. We're not even called mechanics, we're Lube Technicians. We're trained for tire changes, oil flushes, battery replacement and testing, and all the other shit that comes with basic maintenance of an automobile. All the things people could do themselves in twenty minutes.

Markus had stories. Not stories like Benny's which, though tragic to some extent, made us laugh, made us shake our heads and say "what a guy!" Benny had been hooked on ice for six years, had smoked so much in one sitting he'd had a stroke.

"When I woke up, I couldn't move my leg," he said. "So when I start walking again, yeah, I cannot keep my slippah on my foot 'cause no more grip. So I go and just tape 'em."

"Why not just wear shoes?" I asked him.

He looked at me suspiciously, as if I'd said something in an alien and hostile language. Then his wide face broke, mouth with missing molars hacking up a laugh.

"Nah!" he said, hobbling away.

"What a guy, eh?" Normie said as he passed, his wobbly belly caressing my forearm. "Eh Tony, that part come in for the Pontiac? From da kine."

We all had dirty hands all the time, the skin under the grease dried out and split, thin flakes curling out from the webbing between our thumbs and pointer fingers. When I'd first started, I'd wash my hands every two minutes, until I realized it was useless. As soon as you touched the smooth wing nut on an air filter, your hands were no longer clean.

On Markus's big hands, the black oil dust and grease smears covered twice the area of palm. More than once, when things were slow, I saw him massaging the fatty heel of one hand with the thumb of another, as if he could rub the filth out of the whorls and creases. He'd continue to go at it, not even looking at his hands, looking at the wheels of the rolling tool cart.

"What's up, Mark?" Tony said once, after belching an invisible but potent cloud of Pepsi and Portuguese sausage.

Markus's hands dropped to his sides, limp. "Nothing, man. Just my hands hurting."

Another time I stood next to the hood of a 1998 Accord with a carbon receipt in triplicate, explaining to the owner how we'd rotated his tires. While I spoke, the man, distracted, glanced from me to Markus, who stood close to his car, long iron wrench in one hand, tire gauge in the other. His entire body was tense, compressed into itself, jaw so tight a squiggly vein stood out at each temple, hands clenched to fists around the metal instruments he held. I hesitated while pointing to a line on the sheet. The dark circles of Markus's irises had become unnaturally large, so that the entirety of the surrounding white had been swallowed by glossy, absent black.

I put the man into his car and went to Markus. "Is everything all right?" I said, looking up to his twisted, strained face. "Hey Markus. You okay? You okay, man?"

I could almost hear the screech of metal contracting as his grips on the wrench and tire gauge loosened, finger by finger. Then his shoulders went down, dropping into their natural places, and the skin of his face relaxed. Looking down at me he said "There was a time in my life when all I wanted to do was make love to a woman. That's all I wanted to do." He loped back into the garage, and I realized why he rubbed his hands all the time. He held on to the tools too hard.

Later at lunch I saw him towering over the workbench, picking up instruments and studying the blunt or sharp ends of each of them. Normie, a long, crooked train of ash drooping from a brown cigarette filter, his reading glasses perched at the end of his slick nose, sat dismantling a reconstituted alternator. Tony sipped a Gatorade and looked dully toward the garage entrance. Benny, somewhat obsessive-compulsive, stood dabbing at a spot on his blue coveralls, even though I couldn't see the mark anymore. I'd just come back from having parked a Camry for Markus.

"Hey Markus," I said, wiping my hand across my face, "did you make big bucks from all that time in the Middle East?" This kind of thing interested me more than which of his friends died.

"Nah," he said. He looked down at his palms and began to massage the dirt away again. "We got premiums, though. Twenty thousand for a tour in Afghanistan, thirty grand for a tour in Iraq. Another tour, fifty grand."

"Cash in hand?" Tony cried.

"That's right," Markus said. He winced. "One time we were driving through town looking for bomb suspects. They all look the same over there. So we're in our HumVee, you know, and we see this guy in the middle of the road—looks like who we're looking for, right? So we all get out, ready to interrogate. Turns out he's really the chief of police. We're just about to get back in the car when the thing blows up right in front of us."

"So the police chief, uh?" Normie said.

"I could have been a stain, man. So I ask this bastard, who just happened to be in the middle of the road. I ask him, 'Did you know about this fucking bomb?'

"He kind of nods and says, 'Yeah.'

"I'm like, 'Yeah? Then why the hell didn't you say anything?' This is the fucking chief of police, on our side.

"He tells me they were gonna shoot his wife or his kid or some shit, and then he shows us the mine cable, and it leads all the way to the exploding device. Like he wants to be all helpful after he almost killed us."

"What did you do with him after?" I said.

"What we do with all of 'em," he said. He shook his head. "Thing is, I would have probably done the same thing if I was him."

We looked at one another. We all hated the goddamn terrorists and were shocked to hear a veteran saying he would have done the same things as a terrorist.

"But," Tony said.

"Ho, I remember this one time," Benny said, as if he either hadn't been listening to the story at all, or listening too close. "I was driving a limo for this one company. Had liquor in the back—whiskey, champagne, all that shit, yeah? So one night me and my friend, we got all blind and said 'fuck it' and drank everything. Drove all over Waikiki picking up hookers and bums and getting all cracked out."

"Sucking Benny," Normie said, laughing. "You something else, yeah?"

"Was doing doughnuts in the Ala Moana parking lot before the cops came."

Everyone began laughing. "How you do doughnuts in

a limo?" I asked, but no one heard. Markus laughed too, shaking his head. Then he took a deep breath and sighed through his lips, looking at Benny sideways, probably thinking what would it have been like to have a life like that? A life not Iraq, not always near-death, a life with beaches everywhere, with drugs, no guns, just local people with their local people problems.

A week before Markus went back to Atlanta, I saw him standing in the corner of the garage as I came out of the bathroom, the cheap brown paper towels we always ordered dissolving over my wet hands. The older guys were on lunch and we had three cars already come in for new batteries, new tires, oil change, and two more had just pulled up outside. Markus was supposed to have been draining the old oil from a Dodge, but instead he stood facing the wall.

I was hungry. "Markus," I said.

If he heard me he made like he didn't. I stared at his back. I wanted food. I didn't want to be doing all this shit when the guys got back. But I saw a quiver in his high shoulder, a heave in his broad back. Markus was crying.

It wasn't something I've ever seen before or ever expected to see from a grown man, especially Markus. The first thing I wanted to say "It's all right, man. Talk that shit out. Talk it out. It doesn't mean shit." They said things like that in the movies.

I stepped forward. "Markus," I said again. And again no answer. I wadded up the paper towel and threw it in the garbage can. I didn't know what the fuck he was going through and neither one of us had time to pretend that I did know. We weren't a book club, or a support group. We were five guys who came to work with hangovers and liked to bullshit. In a garage, also, the traditional rules of engagement are suspended. With him standing there, I felt time slow down, grow sticky. I wasn't about to get trapped.

"Markus," I said again, this time louder. "This shit ain't gonna fix itself."

Strangers

First, let me tell you about the squatters.

Somebody told me these mainland backpackers had shacked up in the old theater up the road. I'd seen them walking outside around and around the block from the counter a few times. All of them had long hair, in dreads almost, torn t-shirts, crusty black jeans. Once in a while they'd come in for water, maybe bathe at the bathroom sink. It was like a dog had been hosed off over the tile.

The day this all started the milk pitcher's lip had

crusted over with dairy wax, like it had every day. The milk still smelled fine, so I slid the pitcher into the refrigerator at my knees. Bo, coming round the counter with a plastic tub, dumped dishes into a deep sink right of the coffee grounds dump-bucket—a hole really—next to the espresso machine. I wiped at a blotch of dried milk on the counter near the cash register with a rag. I'd been wiping at the spot the whole day.

Bo leaned against the front counter and crossed his arms.

"You know, Albert, I've been thinking."

I looked away into the seating area. The afternoon lull. People thinking was never any good thing. Bright light busted through the wall-sized windows onto textbook covers as university students blinked against the glare of glossy pages and sipped cold coffee. In the corners, the Myspace motherfuckers sucked up the free wireless and chatted with teenage girls.

"I was thinking of having you over at my house one of these days. Maybe tomorrow."

For the past two weeks Bo and I had been drinking beers together at Top of the Hill after work. I knew we were really only strangers working in the same place. Like strangers sometimes do, we just talked about shit hypothetically, for conversation purposes, without being invested in any particular thing. He seemed to want to be my friend. But I had no friends.

"My wife—I was telling her about you—she'd like to have you over for dinner."

"Dinner." I said. "Wife."

"I don't wear this ring for nothing," he said, raising his left hand. There was a pale fade from the rest of his hand around his ring finger. "Oh. I always leave it at home. You know, the sinks."

Randy came out from the kitchen, arms with baking flour up to his elbows. He yanked a cup from a sleeve near the soda fountain and shook his head at the pastry display case while the Coke poured.

"Why are you still here?" Bo said. "Don't we have enough?" He waved at the bread puddings—apple cinnamon, maple, papaya and white chocolate chip, peanut butter/blueberry—each rectangle stacked on little plates next to dried-out scones, oatcakes, droopy muffins, and bundt cakes slick with sugar-water frosting.

"Bread puddings," Randy said, wiping his forearms down in the sink. "No one's gonna eat them. Amy can't make anything else so she keeps making bread puddings. I gotta make things people are gonna eat."

Randy and Amy's baking war—at least how Randy had

described it—started from a butter mochi Randy made one afternoon, when he and Amy worked together for a couple of hours. Amy had taken it personally that the entire pan had sold out in thirty minutes or whatever. I relate this not because I care, but because every time I saw Randy, it was all he talked about.

"She's testing me," Randy said. "But I'm not gonna stoop to her level. Just the basics. No weird shit."

"So what do you think?" Bo said to me. "Tomorrow? After work?"

An hour later, when Bo had already clocked out and my time was up, I folded the bill I'd changed out from the tip jar and slid it into my jeans. I put a cap on the cup of to-go coffee and poured a lemonade. As I went out from around the counter I heard Randy, who should have left at noon, talking to Anna, the evening shift worker. She stacked shelves of bagels, her earrings clicking as they wobbled at her neck. Randy talked at her back. Amy had come in to take free food out of the kitchen, but, seeing Randy, she'd turned and left.

"How come not even a hi or bye?" he demanded, as if Anna had been in the middle of everything the whole time. The stakes of their conflict were still unclear, apparently. "Why she gotta be like that? So you make bad food—no reason to be mad at me."

"That's—crazy," Anna said, thinking about other things.

#

I got off the bus at the hardware store near the end of Waialae, then crossed the street over to Harding, where I stepped over a low stone wall onto the brown grass of someone else's lawn. A Chevy—rust holes in the doors, trunk lid, and bumper—sagged in the driveway, the air all gone from its tires. The house itself was thin wooden planks with brown paint, garage full of broken things. I opened the screen door and went in.

In the living room a breeze through the window screens of the open jalousies pushed around dust and the stiff blades of a ceiling fan. The same breeze rocked the woman in the middle of the living room, in her chair. Her bent body bobbed in front of a television tuned to a children's program. A vacuum hid behind the TV set in the corner. Spaced out on a wall hung painted portraits of green plants. Every time I came into the house I saw a face in those pictures, but looking straight on I saw a plant, faded for sunlight and dust.

A simple hello could set the lady in the rocking chair into spasms. So I went past her, past the kitchen with its wheezing fridge down a corridor where the real faces were-- black and white photos of dead people staring at one another from opposite walls--to an open bedroom door.

Collette, her face and breasts sagging over a small belly, sat on a stool in front of the bedroom mirror, cigarette in an ashtray smoking itself up to the ceiling. The styled wave in her bangs drooped downward. Her eyes were smudged with dark makeup. Collette's tired reflection looked at me as I came in, gave a smile from the eyes only, and blew smoke from the side of its mouth.

"How was work?" she asked, turning her back to the mirror.

"Twenty dollars," I said, pressing the bill into her palm.

"Albert, you don't have to keep—"

"Forget it," I said. "Just woke up?"

"Took a nap," she said, placing the money in one of the vanity boxes in front of her mirror. "Came home, fed mom, ate an ice cream sandwich and fell asleep."

"You probably don't want this lemonade, then."

"Sweetie. Don't be an idiot."

"You can only have it after."

"After what?"

An hour later she stroked my back, my legs over the side of the bed, the bed spread in a crumpled pile at my feet. In her other hand she held the lemonade and sucked at the straw.

"You look worried."

"Bo asked me over to his house for dinner."

"You make it sound like an awful thing. Is he gay or something?"

"He's married."

"So what's the problem? People have dinner all the time. It's a common experience. Mostly painless."

Through the door, now shut, I heard a wet groaning, a throbbing sound from a throat full of phlegm.

"I should put mom to bed," Collette said. She rubbed her fingers hard into her eyes. Makeup dust drifted onto the mattress. "You sticking around?"

"No," I said, going for my clothes around the room.

Collette lifted herself off the bed and put on her underwear, then her exercise pants and a t-shirt. "We should go to a movie some time. That twenty bucks — we could get two tickets."

"Never anything good," I said.

"Well, sometimes people fall in love in the movies. Those are the ones I like the best." She wrapped her mouth around mine, going for a theatrical kiss. She wanted to pretend so I let her pretend.

\#

Bo called me the next day at work and gave me

directions, said I should come over as soon as I got off. When I was done I walked down Waialae a few blocks to the wine store, bought a bottle of red with my tips, and came back up a block on my way to Palolo. He told me he lived in a small house on one of the side streets not far from into the valley. I turned the block at the old Queen Theater and saw the backpackers crossing a parking lot behind the building with boxes in their arms. One of them had bloody scrapes over his arm and one side of his face.

Bo's house was square, painted gray and elevated off the ground about a foot. Four broken concrete stairs led to the front door. I knocked and Bo pulled the door back, smiling. He clapped a hand on my back and pushed me inside.

"Albert!" he yelled. I took off my shoes on a patch of linoleum on the other side of the door. A thick purple carpet spread through the rest of the living room. The linoleum started again at the kitchen, from which a beautiful woman emerged with a wooden salad bowl in both hands. She wore a short cotton dress, her feet bare. A plastic chopstick held her hair up in a bun..

"Sorry!" she said. She'd left something in the kitchen. "We'll be ready to eat in a second."

"My wife," Bo said. "Noelani."

The furniture in the living room and the dining room

had probably come from other people at different times. Behind the stereo system where the television should be a shelf of swollen books leaned into one another.

"Lotta books I just took from the coffee shop," Bo said. "You wanna read one?"

"No thanks," I said.

"Don't read? Come on, Albert, it's good for the soul."

I didn't have anything to say.

Noe returned, set a plate of grain loaf surrounded by an oval of brown gravy on table. She wiped her hands on a dishtowel.

"Noe," she said. "It's nice to finally to meet you, Albert. Bo has told me a lot."

I didn't respond. I wondered what she'd heard.

"Okay," Noe said slowly. She also looked at Bo, nervous. As if she'd done something wrong. "The food's ready—"

The entire meal Noe stared down at her food and broke it into smaller pieces. She nodded when Bo told her something I'd said, or about something we'd both seen at the coffee shop—an old sunburned man who picked at the scabs on his head while he watched *Law and Order* on the big TV.

"I saw those backpackers—those homeless kids or whatever—walking around the Queen Theater," I said to Bo after we'd eaten. Noe ran water over the dishes..

"Backpackers?" Bo said. He pushed his chair back, crossed his legs, and began cleaning his fingernails.

"Yeah, those guys we always see around. Dressed in black."

"Oh yeah? What were they doing?"

"Just walking. They were carrying boxes."

"Were they full?"

"They looked heavy."

"That's good. Good."

"Why good?"

"Brandy and coffee," Bo said, as Noe set cups in front of us. He dusted his hands off and pulled a swollen cigarette wrapped in brown paper from his pocket. After he looked at it a second he held it out to me, along with a red lighter.

"Go ahead," he said. "Be our guest."

Noe took large mouthfuls of coffee, swallowing one after the other.

I pinched the joint a a few times before I put my lips around it and lit it.

We smoked at the table, drinking our coffees in between. Nobody talked. After some kind of signal from Bo, Noe picked up her chair and sat between Bo and me. With her so close, it all became very funny. I was looking straight into

Bo's face. He smiled back at me and nodded, seeing what I'd seen.

Noe's palm slid over the short hairs of my neck and pulled my head into hers. She put her mouth around mine. While she kissed me I looked to Bo, and he smiled again.

#

At Top of the Hill, breaking balls over pool tables sounded over a young guy bent over the bar. "Fuck it all! Fuck it all!" he shouted, slapping the bar with his hand. Nobody could tell what he'd lost or what he hated. So they paid for their Miller Lites and gripped his shoulder and went back to their pool or darts. A few of them shook their heads and moved to the other end of the bar so they wouldn't have to pay attention to him.

Bo got up and sat again, got up and sat, shoving dollar bills into the jukebox on the wall behind the chalk cone, which some of the players used for their hands. He came back, again and again, holding two bottles of beer by their necks.

"So what do you think of the music?"

"What?"

"The music. The songs I'm playing. It's good shit, right?"

"I haven't been listening."

"Come on, man, this shit is golden."

I drank my beer.

The upset guy at the bar jerked to his feet. His stool fell on its side. His glass stayed in his hand, and the beer sloshed over fingers. "I want to die! I just want to die!"

Bo turned around. "Kill yourself, then," he said.

The pool players set the ends of their cues on the floor and leaned forward. A dart wasn't thrown and remained between two fingers. The jukebox went on, a song I didn't recognize.

"Take it easy," one of the men said evenly from across the pool table.

"Getting a little tense in here," Bo said. He swallowed the rest of his bottle. "Come on, I want to show you something."

We came out of the dimness of the bar into the sadder dimness of streetlights and bright signs. Shadows were long and gaping under roofs and between orange lamps high over the street. If the whole world looked like this anyone could do anything and no one would care. Just another part of the scenery. A knife in the gut, a bullet in the brain, would all seem perfectly natural.

We walked toward Bo's house and I felt my hands sweating through the pockets of my jeans. I thought of kissing Noe again, of Bo's arm gripping my forearm, pulling at it, pushing it, controlling me. We hadn't talked about it since it happened.

We stopped at the corner just past the dark, closed Bank of Hawaii. The Queen Theater was in front of us. Its marquee hung on rusted brackets, and its glass doors had been bolted up from the inside with wood. I couldn't see my reflection in the glass, only a glare. That painting of Andre the Giant on the wall above above us was half-covered in shadow, like he wore a blindfold.

Bo put his face to the door. First he tried the handle and began knocking, then punching, then rattling door with his fist.

"Hey!" he yelled. "Fucking let me in already." His voice bounced off the glass and came right back to us.

A few seconds later this loud scraping came from inside, what sounded like a set of metal shelves dragged across a concrete floor. A hand pulled a piece of wood from the other side of the door. The same hand, now more of an arm, gathered the black felt — the same stuff they used to cover fences at construction sites — that had been hung over the glass on the other side. One of the backpackers, his shirt off, in tight black jeans. He twisted a knob and the door came free, squealing out toward us.

The lobby of the gutted theater was lit by a camping

lantern on top of a wooden cable spool. T-shirts and underwear hung over rusted and crumbling building material, most of it old wall. Blankets and foam mattresses had been crumpled into a nest near the spool and its light. On the other side of the lobby, unlit signs that might have displayed popcorn or M and M's had all been beaten to pieces, and the glass display counter was now only a shelf of smashed glass bits that had splashed out through the floor. Over everything I saw the beginnings of messages written in spray paint, most of them in shadow and unreadable.

Two men smoking on top the pile of bedding turned to us.

"What did you take the covering down, for?" Bo said, sliding sideways through the door before me. "The light's still on, and you're taking off the covering. What's wrong with you?"

Under the lamp the two men smiled big and yellow, blowing smoke and clouding the only light in the room.

"I thought," one man began.

"If you thought at all you would have remembered that this is our secret hiding place, asshole. They don't give you a free trip back to the mainland for breaking the law. They put you in prison. And if you think our lovable local inmates would take it easy on mainland haole dumbfucks like you —"

"All right, jeez," the shirtless man said, throwing the cloth back over, trying to catch the edge on a jagged piece of metal over the door.

Beyond the lamp and spool, in another part of the theater, some collection of boards and bars and garbage clattered as it hit the ground, echoing. It had come from the movie theater itself, the room with the screen. Watching the blackness, I saw red hands and a face grow as they moved forward into the lanterns glow, sucking in the lamplight. The fourth man wiped the back of his shiny, sweaty mouth with the back of his shiny, sweaty hand, and stood with the other hand on the spool, looking at Bo.

"Did you come to see the new merch?" the man said, the glitter on his black Led Zeppelin shirt sparkling.

"Sure," Bo said, searching for something in the darkness. "I can't take anything with me now, but show me what you got." Bo pushed away dislodged shelving and stepped on tubes of overhead lights until he found something to sit on, a milk crate he turned over.

"Go ahead, sit down," he said to me, sliding over another milk crate.

"Get the shit," the man standing said, and the two men lounging on blankets flicked their cigarettes away and rolled to their feet.

"God it stinks in here," Bo said, wiping his hands on his thighs. "Where have you guys been using the bathroom? I told you, just go to McDonald's."

The men didn't answer. Then there were three large boxes in front of the wooden spool and the light, and the men all turned to look at Bo.

"This place could use a woman's touch," Bo said. "Well, come on. The suspense is killing me."

One of the men opened his box and pulled out two fistfuls of flat cases, which he fanned out to us. DVD's or video games, I couldn't tell.

"Still wrapped?" Bo said.

"Yep. Good stuff, too."

"Like what? *Legally Blond Two*? *A Walk to Remember*? Fucking faggot. All right, what's next?"

The second man, as proud of himself as the first, showed us shoe boxes—women's shoes. One pair he took from the tissue paper and held up by its straps.

"I bet you knew just what you were looking for, you queer," Bo said. I looked at him—in the shadow I could only see his eyes bright and sick.

The third man had and electronic equipment: laptops, video game machines.

"Nice," Bo said. "I'll take it all tomorrow." He dug a

hand around in a pocket and withdrew a plastic baggie which threw it toward the table. "For now, though, I think it behooves us to enjoy the fruits of our labors." The baggie bounced off the shirtless man's chest before it went to the ground. The three men went to their knees instantly, their fingers sliding over the filthy floor. Their leader, the fourth man, remained standing at the table, holding his hand to his mouth as if inhaling some scent from his wrist. He turned and looked back at the theater from where he'd come.

As soon as they found the baggie the men started smoking a short pipe with a metal bowl. The fog that came at me from the lamp smelled like window cleaner. Unlike the others, the leader slowly took the pipe with its red hot bowl and licked his lips before he inserted the stem between them. The straight blue flame from his pocket torch hissed and smoke leaking out through his nostrils surrounded his face. The cloud was thick as cotton candy and thickened over our heads as he exhaled. He held the pipe out to us. One of the backpacker's eyes bulged and blinked like a frog's. Someone else groaned from the pit of his stomach.

Bo got to his feet and took the pipe. He took a small hit, made a show of enjoying it, and brought pipe and lighter to me.

What came with the inhale coated my tongue, the

inside of my cheeks, my throat, with the sticky, scraping flavor of sugary breakfast cereal, and for the first time since I'd run four blocks for a bus three years ago I could feel I had a heart and that it was not as big as I'd thought. I felt my teeth could bend backwards if they were pushed enough. My chest was a melting piece of hard candy.

The pipe went around and the others talked about things they'd seen at the beach, a topless girl and some asshole wearing a Speedo bathing suit. A nose hair waving in the air inside my nostril. I pulled at it, but nothing was between my fingers when I held them to the lamp.

"Stop that," Bo said, pushing my hands away from my face. "Stop doing that."

"Sorry," I said.

"Fucking animals," he said, looking at the men. They could have been speaking another language. He dug through their boxes, holding DVD covers to the lamp. "Some of this shit just came out."

"What will you do with it?"

"What do you think? I'm going to fucking sell it."

"To who?"

"Who cares? It's not that hard to unload hot merchandise."

Then I heard a voice above everyone else, a cry maybe,

but I couldn't tell. It wasn't from anyone around me—it came from the walls and piles of garbage that separated us from the viewing room. A woman's voice. It only came once, and softly.

"What? You're spacing out, man."

I said nothing. The leader licked his palm and went out of the room, out of the light. I threw the black felt away from the glass door and ran to the street.

At Collette's house I pushed open the door and stepped onto the ratty living room rug with my shoes on. Panels of street lamp glowed orange and weak through uncovered windows on the walls. The pictures of plants, the plants themselves hummed and hissed as they dissolved in the light. I wanted to turn on the television so I wouldn't hear the plants dying. I wanted to turn and leave. The wooden floor of the corridor barked up at me as I stepped through foam to Collette's room. When I pushed open the door the knob smashed loud against the thick white paint of the wall.

Collette lay on the bed in front of me. Baggy t-shit over armless shoulders.

"What? Albert?"

I set one knee on the mattress and put my body over hers My shoes were still on my feet. My hands tore at the buttons of my jeans.

"Shh," I said, covering her mouth with a palm and tightly closed fingers. Her eyes shone blank like television sets turned off. When my pants had been pulled down enough, my other hand went to the bare skin of her soft belly, over her ribs, and held her breast. Her eyes closed.

I felt the air from her nose warm and hard on my knuckles. I pulled my hand away from her mouth.

"Albert? What's wrong?"

After I'd rammed it between her spread legs a few times it hung above her, a small saggy object.

"Albert?"

I pushed off the bed and put it away and left.

Morning time I woke up late, my legs cramped, my feet bent and spread toes locked in place. The sun glared through the window over my bed. I licked my lips but all was sand in my mouth. When I rolled over, the sun burned my back.

I told myself how much it didn't matter that it would have happened whether I was there or not. I crawled off the bed and put my cheek against the wood floor, where it was out of the sun and cool. I belonged there.

#

When the coffee shop closed I was the only one left. I refilled the sweetener at the cream and sugar stand and stored the turning milk in the refrigerator for one more day. My palms were sticky and wrong against the mop handle. The fumes rising up from the mop bucket were of a dead, wet thing. I spread it out, covered the floors with the smell. I went for the dry black milk foam and spilled soda. I'd only finished one side of the floor and I was sweating already.

With the oven, the air conditioning, and the radio off there was only the splash of mop water in the bucket. I was too tired to carry the bucket to the sink and change it out. I didn't notice the knocking on the opposite side of the glass door.

Hardly looking up, I shook my head and waved. The knocking came louder, then they thrashed the door handle. I set the mop into the bucket and looked out the door, said "get the fuck out of here."

Outside stood one of the mainland backpackers, in the same black clothes — the leader.

"We're closed," I shouted.

"I know. Open up. I have something for Bo."

"Why don't you give it to him yourself?"

"I have to get out of town, like right now. Cool out on the North Shore for a couple of days."

"Cool out?"

"Just open the fucking door."

I turned the lock and he was inside, already past me.

"Hey, you wouldn't give a shit if I made a sandwich, would you? Bo said you'd be cool with it."

"What?" He smelled stronger than the mop water. I hated that smell.

"I'm going to make a sandwich," he said.

"Fine," I said. I looked at the floor. I didn't know what hate was. "It's not like it's my food anyway."

I heard him open the walk-in refrigerator in the kitchen, heard the wheels of the sandwich cart. In two minutes he was at the counter dropping crumbs.

"What's your name?" he said. "Wait—I bet it starts with an 'A'."

I wrung the mop into the bucket and looked at him. "Albert. Bo already told you."

"Actually, Bo didn't tell me anything. I'm kind of a psychic. Ask me a question I shouldn't know. Go on. I bet I'll answer it."

"Look, man, I just want to mop this floor and get the fuck out of here." I did a quick once-over through the bathrooms and came back out to the counter.

"Fine. Don't ask me anything. I'll guess anyway." He smiled, the spaces between his teeth spackled with cheese and yellow mustard.

"Eat your heart out," I said.

"You have a woman."

I shook my head and spit in the mop bucket.

"Are you going to eat that sandwich or talk yourself through it? I'd like to get out of here before sunrise."

"I'm right, aren't I? You wouldn't believe the pictures in my mind. I'm getting a name—starts with a K. Kathy. No, something more—Colleen. Collette, right?"

I spat again. "I don't know what the fuck you're talking about."

"You sure?"

"I'm sure."

"Ah, fuck it. It isn't absolutely right all the time." He pushed his empty plate over to me and set his feet back on the wet floor. "You gonna let me out?"

I locked the door behind him and watched him go through the red lights to Queen Theater.

After I'd turned the lock from outside I walked to Bo's house, ready to tell him to fuck himself. And his friends. When I stepped to the door, my fist drawn back and ready to pound, I heard glass shatter against the floor, or a wall. Then came the wet sounds of a hand going hard against a cheek.

"You motherfucking faggot! You ruined the whole thing!"

I hardly recognized Noe's voice. Several more

punches — or kicks maybe — and groans from Bo and I knew he was getting the beating, not giving it.

"I just wanted — you said —"

"I won't do it. I won't! Don't flatter yourself to think you're some goddamn pimp! You're shit!"

Her screaming went quiet as a body went to the floor.

"You do as I say," I heard Bo say. "Don't flatter *yourself* to think you're something better than a whore. You've gone this far, you might as well go the whole way."

Then sobbing.

"Shh. This is fun, isn't it?"

I didn't want to hear any more. I didn't want to stick around. When I thought about it, I hardly knew them.

#

On my day off, Bo didn't show up to work and they called me in. It didn't make any difference. I'd only planned on lying in bed and smoking cigarettes with the ashtray on my chest. Anna stood at the bagel locker sliding new rows of Everythings three by three.

"Did you hear? Lisa fired Amy. She's upstairs right now, going over the money."

"Who?"

"Amy. Lisa fired Amy. The one who kept making bread pudding."

"She got fired for making bread pudding?"

"No, dummy. She was stealing food. Like crazy. Lisa caught her with a foil wrapped package of smoked salmon, salami, and provolone cheese."

"Jesus," I said.

"Good fucking riddance, too," Randy said from behind.

"Why?" I said. "I mean, she wasn't that bad, was she?"

"I don't know," Anna said. "I never even talked to her."

Randy pursed his lips and shrugged, turned back to the kitchen.

A fat man stood on the other side of the register and squinted at the menu board above our heads.

"Yes?" I said.

"You guys got soup?" he said.

"We discontinued the soup."

"No more soup? Ah, that's okay. How's the, what you call it, the mushroom melt?"

"It's fine."

"Just fine?"

"I've never eaten it."

"Well, just put one white chocolate mocha on top the mushroom melt," the man said.

"Hey," I said to Randy. "White chocolate mocha and a

mushroom melt."

"Eight dollars," I said to the man.

He pulled his wallet from his back pocket and the glass door opened behind him. Three of them came in and everyone at the tables stared, whether they were lecturing their table mates with their bullshit or just reading the free magazines. When they saw me they nodded and waved.

"I hate those assholes," the man at the register said. "You know them?"

"No," I said.

"They should lock them up or something. Get them the hell out of here. I know it was them that broke the playground set at the park. I saw them hanging out there the night before they found it like that."

"Yeah," I said.

"Thieves, too. Stuff missing here, there. Somebody should go after them with a gun."

"Eight dollars," I repeated. I took his money and told him to sit down and wait.

While one of them took the bathroom the other poured cups of water from the cooler out in the dining area. After they wrecked the restroom they took a table outside, scraping chairs against the floor, spreading legs, throwing arms over their shoulders, smoking when they weren't supposed to.

"Albert," someone said from behind me. I turned. Lisa stood below me. "Albert, where is the deposit from last night? The money we supposedly made."

"I put it in the safe. I always put it in the safe."

"Well, the money wasn't in the safe."

"I put—"

"You sure you didn't put it somewhere else? I looked everywhere around for it."

"No. I put it in the safe."

"The money wasn't in the safe, Albert. If you can't locate it soon, we're going to have to have a talk."

#

Collette was sitting in her living room when I came into the house, still in her blue work shirt and black pants. She held a plate under her mother's mouth, spooning something soft into it.

"Albert? What's going on? What about work?'

"I don't work anymore."

She wiped her mother's mouth with a napkin and set the plate on the coffee table. "Well, now that you're here, why don't you have a seat and watch TV with us. *The King of Queens* is on."

"Not interested," I said.

I went to her room and opened the drawers under her

mirror, looked in the closet, threw the sheets back. It was the same as it had always been,.

Collette came in quick behind me. "What the hell are you doing? That's my stuff!"

"He said your name! He said your fucking name! How do you know him?"

"Albert, calm down —"

I took the bed frame in both hands and flipped it completely over. The mattress bounced against the wall before turning over on the floor.

"Those fucking backpackers--what the fuck are they to you?"

"Are you out of your mind?"

"Stop lying!" My half-closed fist went to her jaw; she staggered backward but didn't fall, her makeup stand and open drawers stopping her. The mirror tilted forward until it fell back into place. I put my hands up. For a second she looked at me, her eyes showing more white than I'd ever seen, her mouth a gaping hole.

"Come on," I said, keeping my hands up in fists.

She didn't come at me with the hair curler, the jewelry box, her hand mirror. She touched the red mark on her face, tears falling over her fingers. "Don't, please," she said softly.

It wasn't her fault.

\#

Before I broke into Queen's Theater I walked out to those beaches around Kahala, the backyards of those glass mansions, with patios built on the first floor roofs. I fell down on the shore. I pissed in the bushes and walked back up the hill towards Kaimuki.

No one cared that I'd come in. Three of them weren't there, the last one shirtless and wearing shades, kneeling in front of a new boom box on the floor, turning the volume loud then soft then silent. Then loud then soft then silent.

"Nuts," he said, without seeing me.

I stepped toward him and stopped when I saw Bo on his back on the floor, boards still with nails underneath him. When the shirtless one turned down the volume I heard, from the theater, the barking of the other three, the pleading of a woman.

I grabbed Bo by the shirt and pulled him up. Even in the dim light I saw eyes rolling in sockets. He laughed at the back of his throat.

"Didn't mean—"

The boards slapped against his body after I let him go. The backpacker turned to me. He said nothing—he smiled and turned the volume up on the radio until the distorted noise was the only sound in the theater. I took a piece of clipped rebar and walked by him into the viewing room.

Around the bright fire of a kerosene lamp the shadows were tall and torn, things to be impaled upon. The ragged slit down the middle of the movie screen opened and closed like a winking eye. The chairs had been pulled from their places, some stacked on one another. In the middle aisle the lamp glowed on four naked bodies, the skin of each one sick and orange and greasy and tangled. All tangled in a mess—I couldn't tell whether they were feeding or fucking.

Five immortal souls trapped to a world together and this was how we used up our time. I never felt my soul so keenly as when I knew it was ready to depart. From the other room I heard the radio clearly.

We might have all been brothers in another time, we might have laughed and sang songs together. But here we didn't know one another and we didn't know ourselves. We were doomed to live as strangers and die as the same.

I took the hair of the woman full in my hand and threw her to the shadows. She might have been Noe, she might have been Collette. It didn't matter. She was every woman who had gone unloved. When they leaped at me, I brought the end of rebar down on skulls and jawbones and I thought I am killing him, I am killing me, I am killing all of us.

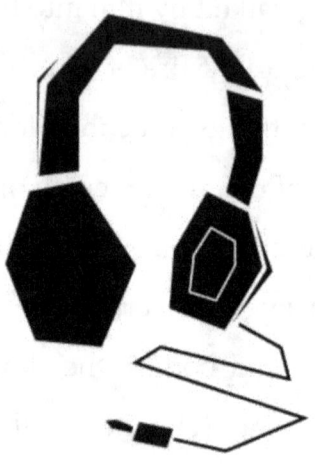

Psychic Cannibal

The Psychic Cannibal had no business going on the radio that night. Wobbling from the 7-11 past the athletic complex and the lower campus pool, up the stairs that led who-knew-where, pausing at the crosswalk to catch his breath. He'd wobbled so bad the coffee he'd brought from the bottom whence he'd emerged was mostly out of the cup and streaming warm down his fingers.

Some electric device in the machinery of the traffic lights ticked slowly when the light was red, and went crazy when green came around. There were no cars on the road anymore, wouldn't be for hours.

The wobbling wasn't just the leg he'd wrecked weeks ago when he'd flown, like trash, from his bike onto the cracked asphalt of a parking lot, edges and sharp lips and ground cement and broken glass. Earlier that night he'd been tanking bomber after Newcastle bomber, topped off by a blunt as heavy as a nickel. Even after he crossed over the street to the tune of a monkey beating recklessly on a toy drum, fear overtook chemical oblivion and smeared a clammy gel over his back. The Psychic Cannibal knew cars don't just come from nowhere. And yet sometimes they did.

Most people called him Jann.

And he usually referred to himself as Jann, except when he proclaimed himself the Psychic Cannibal into the bulbous foam head of a radio mike smelling of bad breath and curry. "I am the Psychic Cannibal, and you are listening to 'Bygones Be Bygones' on KTUH-FM Honolulu. The next three hours will be bereft of semblance or resemblance, expunged of hypotheticals and theoreticals. Engorged with the tactile curvature of the Now. It is not dying. It is never dying."

It was ten minutes to midnight.

The stars, dim as they were, were now too near above him. The light from the shut-up campus buildings scraped his skin every time he limped into their dim, terrifying illumination.

There was only one time when drinking excessively and inhaling a generous pinch of weed had made him feel good.

As he neared the radio station (second story above the cafeteria, down the hall from the dental clinic), he felt no pain, just a vague sickness comprised of the overwhelming dimness, the occasional burst of orange light from roofs of closed offices, and the shadows by which the world was meshed. All that he could make out concerning how he felt was what he saw. And that was: Betsy was gone, gone, that she'd loved him and stitched him up and put him on his way. She'd stayed for the worst of it: the accident, the nursing, the errands, the reading of his "Between the Wars: Fitzgerald and Hemingway" texts until he could open both eyes and read them on his own. Then their parting was as swift as Nick Adams's before The Three-Day Blow."

If she could only see me at my best. The Psychic Cannibal thought this kind of thing frequently because there was, especially at this moment, no other way to think. If only she could see me less sniveling, less needy, less broken. It was the slightest variation on what he'd been thinking while he got drunk the previous few hours, listening to the same song on his record player, trying and failing to inject himself with the love of which there was no longer a true source. Betsy was gone, gone.

\#

The studio was locked as it always was after hours. To enter, he had to push a green button that would flash a bright light over the control board, letting the on-air DJ know someone was outside. The Psychic Cannibal leaned with his whole weight on his index finger against the button until the paint-chipped door stickered over in the most random bullshit swung open.

"The Psychic Cannibal," Sugarmouth Crossbreed exhorted, his tiny bearded body backlit and framed by shelves of CDs and records. He lifted his hand as if to clap the Psychic Cannibal on the shoulder, but the Cannibal recoiled.

"Hey Ben," the Psychic Cannibal said. He sidled into the room and into the light. He saw Sugarmouth's hairy, gooey face tighten and his eyes avert from the Cannibal's numb profile.

"Oh, man, I heard you was in a bad way." Sugar walked ahead of him through a corridor of shelves to the control room. "Glad to see you back, man."

The KTUH studio was two turntables on a counter, CD players on top of one another in a rack, a computer that played sound files, all equipment feeding into a smudged control board with busted lights alternating in cues, programs, studio, on and off. There was little the board itself could tell a body—you had to get to know it by feel. On the walls: a matrix of shows in three-hour blocks with scribbled and generally awful show markers, disclaimers for adult content, legal ids, station identifiers, and a multi-layered gatefold of Isaac Hayes' *Black Moses* album spread out into the shape of the cross.

"What, no stash today?"

"Just gonna tap into the vault tonight," the Psychic Cannibal replied.

"Hang on a sec. Let me get on here."

Sugarmouth slipped a pair of misused cans over his hair and hit a seemingly defunct mike button.

"Ladies and gentlemen, that was Harold Melvin and the Blue Notes, my man Teddy Pendergrass on led power growl with 'I Miss You.' Stay tuned for—that's right, ladies and gentlemen, he's back, the man with the tan, the boss with no hearing loss, the return of the Psychic Cannibal, out for— what was it brother, six weeks?"

"Yeah."

Sugarmouth waited a second. Nothing forthcoming. "Six weeks, ladies and gentlemen, and he's back to lay down the hard cuts all the way to three a.m. I will feel you, my children next week—and until then, here's Maze." He punched a button, turned and removed his headphones.

"All yours, man. You mind throwing that one back?" He pointed to a record sleeve on the counter, the shape of a palm made from the curving rows of a labyrinth.

"No problem."

"It's got seven minutes." He raised his hand. "I'm out."

After a few delayed seconds—the Psychic Cannibal wasn't sure if Sugarmouth was several feet away, or all the way hairy cheek to scarred cheek up to him—the Cannibal held out his good hand, and Sugarmouth slapped it.

For longer than it felt, he stood unmoved after Sugarmouth exited through the back door, the Maze record unheard yet revolving nearer its terminus. At last, when it seemed to him all the sound was going away, circling and circling into the void, the Psychic Cannibal stirred. The fade out, he would have called it, were he not fucked as he was.

Relying more on muscle memory than sight, the Cannibal threw a couple dozen sound files into a cue on the computer. A few minutes to get some records together. The song creeped funk-wise to finality as the Psychic Cannibal raised his good hand (though he saw two hands before him) over two glowing buttons that would trigger the computer. As long as two hands hit two buttons, sound would emerge. If only the three out of the four necessary components worked, he was surely insane. The final shreds of sonic material left were softly torn from the still spinning disc. Or had the song ended long ago? That's it, Old Sport, he told himself, as Gatsby would have done.

The fingers hit correctly.

"And now, the KTUH campus event calendar."

The Psychic Cannibal swigged again at his cool coffee and walked with the trepidation of a blind man to the record vault. Rows and rows of LP's, spines broken and fraying and taped, sorted by overlapping genres in no pattern he'd have been able to ascertain if he was sober. The room spun, and the vague sickness from outside now burst from his bowels like a slime creature from the sewers, laying over his brain the thick residue of nausea. If he did not focus he could not see — if he did focus, it was all vertigo and barf. The Cannibal employed a sort of glance through one eye to see what he was doing, and pawed through shelved records until he found three or four.

Setting the records on the turntable was its own challenge, but the Psychic Cannibal knew the records well and what grooves said what. When the last of the announcements played from the computer, he triggered a turntable, hardly recalling what he'd set there in the first place.

A saxophone, alarming in its sonic palpability, came forth first, buoyed by a piano and slight drums in three/four time. The sax threaded in and out of his soul. No, he had no soul, it threaded in and out of his center organs. No — but something was jarred and something moved within him from one note to the next. "Good thing, good thing, good thing, good thing," backup singers mocked over and over and over again.

"You'll Lose a Good Thing," was what he wanted to say to Betsy. A good thing. What was it that old Hemingway said? People are broken in places and put back together and are stronger for it. But those were people who'd been brave. Jann had been broken only because he'd been careless, riding his bicycle with his hands swinging at his sides, his iPod with "Gypsy" on repeat.

He closed his eyes and the world spun without even a fixed reference point about which to spin. He kept swallowing because his teeth sweated. He thought he could stand over the studio garbage can, but was sure he'd plunge headfirst inside it. As the song collapsed upon itself, he started a new turntable. The new song started halfway through the previous number. But at least it gave him a little more time.

Getting to the restroom from the studio was already complicated. For the Psychic Cannibal, it now took on the aspect of a satanic torture ritual. Since all doors had to be locked at all times after hours, he had to prop the door open with a too-long two-by-four that lay under one of the CD shelves. The Cannibal didn't recall the essential piece of wood until the studio door almost closed completely behind him. The tips of his fingers were all that prevented a total shut-out. In anger and pain the Psychic Cannibal kicked at the door with the exposed toes of his rubber-slippered feet. He miscalculated the arc of the swinging door, and as he rushed back into the studio, the now-closing-again door caught him square on the forehead.

This entire charade might have been tolerable had not the Cannibal the overwhelming urge to throw up. With smarting fingers he fumbled with the long piece of wood and when he had a handle at last, dropped it between the crack of the closing door.

Sugarmouth hadn't lifted the toilet seat. Thus it was a yellow-on-white palette to which the Psychic Cannibal added his own ungodly rainbow. The more he smelled his own matter, the more he expelled. The more he expelled, the better he felt. His heart was pinched at the ends and twisted until he was through.

Hem and Scott never wrote about those parts. With everyone drunk as they were all the time, where were the bathroom scenes? Or did they believe if a man tossed his cookies with no one waiting outside to piss, it never really happened?

How easy it would be to believe this wasn't happening. How easy to believe Betsy was waiting for him outside. How easy to believe he hadn't been almost killed, and that his leg might work all the way one day. How easy to believe that Fitzgerald wasn't a moony drunk, or Hemingway a bitchy opportunist, or Gatsby a bootlegger and a hood. Or that music meant anything more to him than it did two hours ago.

The Psychic Cannibal was now among the bacteria, collapsed in a bathroom stall, back against the wall, temples resting on the cool metal of a toilet paper dispenser. The record he'd played partially broke through the open studio door and reverberated around him, against the ceramic white tile. He hadn't even realized what he'd put on until he heard it at that moment: "Hare Krishna" by Marion Williams. The gospel singer. If only it had meant something more now he was paying attention. In the old days, he would have followed the track with "Father Death," Allen Ginsberg barking along to his harmonium. His throat hurt. Slowly he reached for the handle to flush what he could not look at.

When he got back to the studio, face wet and mouth rinsed, the song over the turntable still played at the exact point he'd identified in the bathroom, its insidious repetitions intensified by the pulsing strobe of some pale light reflected in the window between the studio and the record vault. Finally, everything was truly fucked — the only explanation was extraterrestrial.

No, it was the phone ringing, a bulb lighting intermittently so that DJs could see if they could not hear.

"Hello?" the Psychic Cannibal whispered into the receiver.

Where once was drunkenness and sickness was now horror. Nobody called a radio station this late. It was probably that midnight person right outside the door, with a special gift. "Hello," he said again, hearing only the repeated refrain of "Hare Krishna" in the background, echoed a half second later by what he heard over the line. "Hello? Just tell me who's there!" Though the record still played behind him, a crest of feedback washed over the earpiece until he heard nothing again, or the same thing he'd been hearing but miles away. Or maybe right outside the door.

The Psychic Cannibal punched a button and lifted the audio to place the call live over the air. If he was to be murdered tonight, let the whole world hear it. That is, if the whole world outside hadn't already been slaughtered by poisoned gas. How easy it would be to believe that. The

Psychic Cannibal, the Sole Survivor, with No One at the other end of the line.

"Hello, KTUH, you're on the air," he said, his voice quivering. "Caller, you're on the air. This is KTUH!"

For several moments the Psychic Cannibal heard "Hare Krishna" wavering with the modulated ebb and flow of feedback. Then the sound of chewing.

"Oh, sorry man, I totally forgot I was calling." A voice buried in teeth and food. "Um, yeah, I think the record is scratched." Dial tone.

The Psychic Cannibal pushed the microphone away, cut the phone line, tapped the record player once. The needle hopped from outward circle to inner, and the first chorus disappeared into memory or oblivion. He walked backward away from the music and sat down in the studio's single chair.

He didn't say they became stronger, the Cannibal told himself. When people broke in places and were fixed they were never as strong as they once were. When "Hare Krishna" ended he'd usually follow it up with "Father Death," a happier tune than the title would suggest. His eyes grew heavy where he sat. Sooner or later, a light would flash above the console, someone outside the door to relieve him.

So Betsy didn't love him anymore. It was nobody's fault. That didn't sound right. It was everyone's fault, wasn't it? That sounded worse. The Psychic Cannibal closed his eyes. It's my fault, he said, or thought he said. And even though it wasn't ever 100 percent true, it was as close as he was going to get tonight. "It's my fault," he said aloud, and he opened his eyes, thinking he was back in his apartment, Betsy sleeping in the bed. A whistling went through his head, though he couldn't tell if something was being let out or in. As the song wound up, he stood and put the cans on.

About the Author

Jeffery Ryan Long lives in Honolulu, Hawai'i

www.ingramcontent.com/pod-product-compliance
Lightning Source LLC
Chambersburg PA
CBHW071206260626
47162CB00004B/1189